He meant it to be an easy brush of lips, a nibble at most.

A quick, simple and nonverbal statement of intent—assuming, of course, that she didn't smack him away. But then they were connected and she made one of those sounds that women do. It was a coo, raw and sexual, and it sent him over an edge he hadn't even known was there. He pulled back, shaken and burned, and stared at her. *Livia.*

He *wanted* her.

Tightening his grip, he pulled her in again, devouring her this time without any need or ability to be gentle. She made it easy for him, opening her sweet mouth and slipping her tongue into his.

Someone moaned; it was impossible to tell who because there was no separation between them. Nothing but a perfect, seamless whole. And when he found himself delving into her hair, caressing her back and reaching around to pull her writhing hips against his, he let her go because the time wasn't ripe.

But, he now knew, the time would definitely come.

Books by Ann Christopher

Kimani Romance

Just About Sex
Sweeter Than Revenge
Tender Secrets
Road to Seduction
Campaign for Seduction
Redemption's Kiss
Seduced on the Red Carpet

ANN CHRISTOPHER

is a full-time chauffeur for her two overscheduled children. She is also a wife, former lawyer, and decent cook. In between trips to various sporting practices and games, Target and the grocery store, she likes to write the occasional romance novel, always featuring a devastatingly handsome alpha male. She lives in Cincinnati and spends her time with her family, which includes two spoiled rescue cats, Sadie and Savannah, and a rescue hound, Sheldon.

If you'd like to recommend a great book, share a recipe for homemade cake of any kind, or suggest a tip for getting your children to do what you say the *first* time you say it, Ann would love to hear from you through her Web site, www.AnnChristopher.com.

ANN CHRISTOPHER

Seduced on the Red Carpet

KIMANI™
ROMANCE

To Richard

KIMANI PRESS™

ISBN-13: 978-0-373-86181-1

Recycling programs
for this product may
not exist in your area.

SEDUCED ON THE RED CARPET

Copyright © 2010 by Harlequin Books S.A.

www.kimanipress.com

Printed in U.S.A.

Dear Reader,

Vintner Hunter Chambers of the Chambers Winery is a simple man. A widower, he grows his grapes, makes his wine and raises his daughter. Period. That's who he is and what he does, and he doesn't want—or expect—anything else.

Until supermodel Livia Blake steps off the red carpet and into his life.

Suddenly, this enthralling and complicated woman is bewitching everyone in the Napa Valley, including Hunter's daughter and his dog. Misguided Hunter first thinks that he can ignore his growing feelings for her, and then, when that fails, deludes himself into thinking she's not the perfect woman for him.

Poor guy! Why does he have to make things so hard on himself?

I hope you enjoy watching Hunter fall so crazy in love he can't even see straight....

Happy reading!

Ann

Chapter 1

Livia Blake consulted her list again and surveyed the small, neatly packed and nondescript suitcase on her bed. No Louis Vuittons for this little trip to Napa Valley, no, siree; if you didn't have to make a grand entrance to impress the loitering paparazzi, you didn't need the expensive luggage. Nor did you need twenty bags crammed with false eyelashes, hairpieces, stilettos and tiny little black dresses that showed off your freshly waxed legs, so she hadn't packed them.

This getaway was, for once, solely for pleasure. No business. At. All.

Ha!

For the next several days, she could—and would—eat and drink whatever the hell she wanted without worrying about fittings and disapproving remarks regarding the amount of junk in her trunk or her buoyant cleavage (all natural, thank you very much) refusing to be strapped into a postage-stamp-sized bathing suit top. There would be no swaggering runway walks for her, no fake smooches with egomaniacal designers and no over-the-top parties filled with airhead celebrities, socialites or steroid-puffed professional athletes trying to get into her panties.

That's right. She wasn't traveling to the Chambers Winery as Livia Blake, Supermodel. Until she had to report to Mexico for the photo shoot at the end of the month, she was plain old Livia Blake, civilian. Hallelujah.

But the question was: Had she packed everything?

Back to the list.

Hiking boots? Check. Bug spray? Check. Sweaters for those cool northern-California nights? Check. Also in her bag? A satisfyingly thick wine-tasting book, because she didn't want to look like an idiot in wine country; her jogging shoes, because, although she wanted to eat and drink while on vacation, she didn't want to gain thirty pounds while doing so; and her Jackie Robinson biography, which she was *finally* going to finish. She did love her some baseball.

Did she need thicker socks, though? And should she throw in one nice dress just in case—?

The muffled bleat of her cell phone came from somewhere in the room.

Uh-oh. Where was it?

Scrambling for the remote, she hit Pause on the

DVR (she'd been watching *The Dog Wrangler* in the background and wanted to hear what he had to say about the neurotic poodle with stress incontinence) and listened again. Aha. Nightstand. Unearthing it from beneath a pile of rejected scarves, she saw that it was her friend Rachel Wellesley—probably calling about her flight time and when she'd meet Livia at the winery—and clicked it on.

"What's up, girl?" Livia said.

There was no reciprocal greeting. Just a direct launch into the purpose of the call. "We *might* have a problem," Rachel told her.

It always made Livia nervous when Rachel used that easy-breezy tone. "Problem as in you broke a fingernail or problem with the trip?"

During the long pause that followed, Livia saw all of her vacation hopes—the walks along the river to enjoy the fall foliage, the five-star accommodations, the wine tastings—go up in a spectacular plume of black smoke.

After a good two or three beats, Rachel cleared her throat, an additional stall tactic that didn't fool Livia for a second. "Possibly with the trip."

Oh, no. No, no, no. NOOOOOO. No one was going to rain on her parade and spoil the first official vacation she'd had in years. "Spit it out, Rach."

"We can't come," said Rachel.

"What?"

"Not yet, but—"

"Why not?"

"—we want you to go ahead anyway. We'll meet you there when filming's finished."

"Filming was supposed to be finished *today*."

"Trust me, I know. But what can we do? And like I said, you go on ahead. Start without us."

Wow. She had a comedian on her hands. "Will you kindly explain how I'm supposed to start without you when the whole purpose of this little trip is for you to see your fiancé's family winery and decide if you want to get married there? Do you want me to try on wedding dresses for you while I'm at it?"

"Someone woke up on the wrong side of crabby today, didn't they?"

Livia had to snort at that. Staring at her suitcase, she thought about her options.

Option 1: she could sit here on her butt and wonder if she should have her walls repainted.

Option 2: she could take herself to Napa, sightsee, eat and drink to her heart's content and wait for her friends to arrive in a few days. Then they could all eat and drink together.

Okay. Decision made.

"Fine," Livia said ungraciously. "I'll go by myself, but I'm not going to like it."

"Please forgive me."

"No," Livia said, smiling.

"Look at it this way," Rachel said with all the nauseating smugness of a happily engaged woman who could look forward to an orgasm or two that night when she went to bed with her sexy man, "maybe you'll meet someone nice while you're there."

Livia balanced the phone on her shoulder and went back to searching for socks, which was hard to do since she'd rolled her eyes to the top of her head. Meet someone nice? Puh-lease. Nice men were rarer than white tigers on the moon.

"Right. And maybe Donatella Versace will feature a plain white cotton dress with flat shoes during fashion week."

They both got a kick out of that unlikely image.

Napa Valley was, in a word, spectacular.

Having traveled all over the world, Livia didn't use the word lightly, but it applied here. Whereas Las Vegas was spectacular in a tacky, glittery sort of way, and the Great Wall of China was spectacular in a humbling, majestic sort of way, Napa was spectacular in a quietly peaceful way. The gentle mountains, the waves of green trees now speckled with fall orange and the acres of lush vines—row after row, some red (red grapes, she'd read), some gold (white grapes), marching as far as her eye could see and seemingly past the horizon—all touched something deep in her spirit. This was a place that felt like it'd been transplanted from a previous century, and she wouldn't be surprised if its lazy grace made the hands on her watch move a little more slowly than they did in New York or L.A.

This was, in short, a place she could love.

Once she got checked in to the guesthouse, that was.

She parked her rental behind the main bed-and-breakfast, which was wedged into a hillside and larger than she'd expected, and popped the trunk for her luggage. The charming redbrick building had several gables and chimneys and—oooh, she liked those!—pretty little flower boxes at every window, all of which were filled with cheerful red blooms. Several guesthouses, one of which she assumed was hers, were scattered nearby, and there was a—

Oh, wait. Was that a little girl?

It was, about twenty feet away, peering around a tree at her. She was brown-skinned and cute, about five or six, with a head full of dark twists, a white T-shirt with blue shorts and a red bandage on one knee. Could she be any cuter?

"Hello!" Livia smiled and waved. She was never quite sure about greeting strange children because she knew they'd all been taught not to talk to strangers. Hopefully she didn't look too threatening. "Hello," she called again. "My name is—"

The girl scampered off, disappearing around the corner of the big house. Livia watched her go, trying not to get her feelings hurt. Well. So much for new friends, eh?

Yeah, she thought as she bent to grab her suitcase. She loved it here.

Something moved right behind her and smacked her in the butt. She shrieked, jumped, whirled and found herself face-to-face with a pony-sized creature who'd made himself at home sniffing her private parts.

Another shriek welled in her throat, gathering steam, and her frantic brain was wondering how many of her four limbs he could rip off and devour before help arrived, when something weird happened. The thing backed up a couple of steps, cocked his head and studied her with benign interest. Probably not typical predator behavior, true, but that was no reason not to scream. She opened her mouth nice and wide and—

Hold up. That wasn't a pony. It was a dog. The world's biggest and possibly goofiest dog.

Snapping her jaws shut, she stared at the animal, who stared back. The darn thing's head was well past her waist, which was quite impressive since she qualified for Amazon status at five feet eleven inches. He had big brown eyes, floppy ears, knobbly knees and gangly legs that made him look like the canine equivalent of a high school geek. His fur was the kind of brown with black slashes that the Dog Wrangler called—what was it?—a brindle pattern.

A Great Dane. That's what he was. So. Was he going to eat her or not?

Apparently not. He had his big black nose working already, sniffing her, and she knew he'd like what he smelled because her signature fragrance was a light and lovely honeysuckle. Deciding to risk it, she reached out past his broad snout and scratched his ears. They were surprisingly silky, and the dog all but grinned at her in gratitude.

What a sweetie! He wasn't so bad—

Without warning, the dog began barking at her, and each bark was the rough equivalent of a kibble-smelling cannon blast right in her face.

Bark! Bark-bark! BARK!

This pissed her off. One second ago they'd been new BFFs and now he wanted to take her head off for absolutely no reason? Uh-uh.

Calling on the thousands of hours of *The Dog Wrangler* that she'd watched over the years, she stood her ground, arched her fingers into a claw and gave the dog a quick jabbing zap right on his hindquarters. Just like that—*zap!*

This startled the dog, thank God, and he shut up midbark. Better than that, he yelped, backed away, dropped to his belly, rested his snout on his front paws and eyed her with newfound respect, almost as though he was waiting for her next command.

Nodding with grim satisfaction, she put her hands on her hips and stared down at him, daring him to try anything funny with her ever again.

That's right, pooch. Don't you mess with me.

"Hey!" Running feet came up behind her, crunching on the gravel. "What'd you do to my dog?"

What? Was this clown for real? She's almost mauled by a schizophrenic Great Dane and then *she* gets blamed for making the dog behave? Again—uh-uh. Not gonna happen.

"Excuse me," she said, turning and letting the sarcasm

fly, "but maybe you didn't notice that Marmaduke here is a menace to society and—oh."

Whatever else she'd been about to say disappeared in a tiny little *poof!* when she locked gazes with the owner of that booming voice and those feet, who was clearly an asshole at heart hiding behind the body and face of a god.

The first thing she noticed was his height. He was taller—*taller!*—than she was, which was an event so rare in the non-NBA population that it might have been a full solar eclipse during a leap year. But he wasn't a beanpole, which she could clearly see because he filled out his Chambers Winery powder-blue polo shirt and khakis in spectacular fashion, with squared shoulders, heavy biceps, a flat belly and narrow hips that told her, quite plainly, that he spent a little time lifting weights when he wasn't honing his skills at being a world-class jerk.

He was brown-skinned and clean-shaven, with skull-trimmed black hair and eyes that blazed copper fire at her in the late morning sun. Unsmiling, he shifted his accusatory gaze between her and the dog at her feet. She had the nagging feeling that he was sorry the dog hadn't finished her off and planned to do the job himself.

Okay, Livie. Put your eyes back in your head and get a grip.

"That dog—" she pointed to the offender lest there was any confusion about the dog in question "—needs to be on a leash."

Mr. Personality, apparently deciding not to waste any

unnecessary words on her, responded by raising one heavy eyebrow and holding up a black leash for her to see.

"Great." Mollified but still irritated, she matched him glare for glare. "Are you planning to use it anytime soon?"

"If you don't mind."

His exaggerated politeness scraped across her nerves like tree bark. Still glowering, she stepped aside, gave him a be-my-guest flick of her hand and watched to see if he had any dog skills.

He didn't. Inching closer with a wariness that was an open invitation to the dog to cull this weak member from the pack, he reached out with the leash, ready to clip it on the dog's collar.

The dog's head came up. One side of his black-lipped mouth pulled back just far enough to reveal a white incisor that looked sharp enough to mince walrus hide, and the beast emitted a rumbling growl. The man froze, arm outstretched. Livia froze, too, and the dog wasn't even looking at her; she'd heard less fearsome growls coming from the lionesses on Animal Planet shows as they ripped hapless wildebeests to shreds.

The man, his cheeks coloring with either blind terror or embarrassment, shot a glance at Livia and took a minute to regroup. Then he cleared his throat, licked his lips and tried another tactic.

"Nice doggy," he began. "I've got a cookie for you, you big monster, if you let me—"

Another growl, this one punctuated by the flattening

of the hound's ears and the revelation of several more teeth.

Oh, for God's sake. Hadn't this guy ever seen *The Dog Wrangler?* He was doing it all wrong and she didn't have the inclination to watch the dog toy with him any longer.

"Here," she snapped, snatching the leash from his hand.

"Wait—"

The dog tilted his head in her direction and tried that growling nonsense again, but she'd had enough. Snapping her fingers at him, she held her index finger down in his face.

"Hey," she warned, keeping her voice low and calm.

The dog immediately dropped his head back on his paws and stared up at her with dewy eyes, as though he'd been waiting all his life for someone to appear, seize power and become the undisputed leader of his pack. Taking advantage of this peaceful moment, she clipped the leash onto his collar and handed it off to the man.

"That's how it's done." Since the man didn't know she'd never leashed a growling dog before in her life, she didn't bother keeping the smugness out of her voice. "No need to thank me."

The man clenched his jaw in the back, and she waited to hear the snap of his teeth breaking. "Like I said—what did you do to my dog? He doesn't behave for anyone."

Sooo…wait. He hadn't been accusing her of abusing the animal?

"I just, ah, tried to be assertive with him. Let him know who's in charge. You know."

"I don't know, actually." His jaw loosened but he still seemed grudging with his words. "Thanks."

"You should watch *The Dog Wrangler.*"

"Right," he said sourly.

Wow. This guy and his dog both needed attitude adjustments. Big-time. Raising her brows—was there something bitter here in the water in Napa or what?—she turned back to her open trunk and suitcase.

"I'll just take my bag and check in—"

"Let me." Before she could object, and she planned to object because she hated it when overzealous bellhops or doormen snatched the bags out of your hand in their relentless quest for a big tip, even when you could clearly handle the bags yourself, he reached for her bag. "I'm happy to help."

She studied his grim face. "I can see that. But really, I've got it."

Ignoring her, he set the bag on the ground and walked around to peer inside the car's window for who knew what. Seeing nothing but empty car, he looked back up the drive, as though he expected the imminent arrival of someone or something.

"Where's the rest?" he asked.

"Of what?"

"Your luggage? Your entourage?"

Oh. Oh, okay. She got it. He, like other idiots world-wide, assumed that because she was a famous model, she was a diva-licious bitch. Or maybe he'd read some of her press coverage from back in the day, when she was young and stupid, and thought she was still as big an airhead as she'd ever been. Whatever. Clearly he needed a little schooling in both manners and customer service relations, and she was just the woman to do it.

"I take it you know who I am."

Nothing at all changed in his expression, but the quick skim of that light brown gaze down her body and back up again all but ignited sparks across her skin.

"Every man who's ever bought the Swimsuit Issue knows who you are."

Livia froze, her pulse galloping away like a bee-stung horse, because she realized, with sudden excruciating clarity, that this man was trouble. Men checked her out all the time, which was no big deal. She was used to and impervious to it.

This was different.

This was the subtle peeling away of her cute little capri pants and fluttery top. There was banked heat in those eyes, as if he could look at her now and see her as she'd appeared on that *Sports Illustrated* cover when she was nineteen: sun-kissed and dewy, wearing a white triangle scrap of a bikini bottom with the strings undone and dangling on one side, and a loopy crocheted top that displayed every inch of her upper body—except for her nipples—in vivid detail. She'd had her windblown hair in her face, her hips cocked to one side, her lips and thighs parted, and sand dusted across one side of her body while the blue waters off Fiji lapped in the distance.

She'd been a young dingbat then, but as beautiful as she'd ever been—or probably ever would be—in her life. This man, whoever he was, remembered all that. He'd looked at that cover shot and now thought he knew her, but he knew nothing about the girl inside that shell.

Men never did, and she was used to their snap judgments.

What she wasn't used to was the responsive curl of heat in her belly and the tug she felt toward this jerk, as though she'd been secretly magnetized and he was the North Pole.

Shake it off, girl.

"You might know who I am," she said, painfully aware that her Georgia accent was thickening the way it always did when she was upset, so that *might* became *maht* and *I* became *Ah,* "but you don't know me. I don't travel with an entourage when my job doesn't require it, and I only brought one suitcase." She snatched it up from the ground before he could touch it again. "And I will carry it myself."

Propelled by her wounded dignity, she stalked off toward the house, well aware of the surprised widening of his eyes. She'd put several feet between him and his mangy dog when he spoke again.

"Whatever you want."

The subtle mockery made something snap in her brain, covering her vision with red. Halfway to a graceful exit, she discovered that she couldn't let this jackass have the last word. It just wasn't in her.

So she marched back up to stand in his face, suitcase in tow, and pointed her free index finger right at his perfectly straight nose. "You're very rude," she informed him. "You better believe I'm going to complain to the owners about you."

To her further annoyance, this pronouncement only amused him, if the slow smile creeping across his face was any indication. "You do that," he said. "They've had problems with me before. Make sure you tell them my name's J.R."

It would have been so nice to smack that wicked smirk right off his face and teach him a thing or two about the right way to treat a) women and b) paying guests, but that would have required moving and she found she couldn't do that. There was something so sexy about this man, so unabashedly masculine and unaffected, that he made her breath hitch and her heartbeat stutter. And that was something that athletes, actors and rock stars alike hadn't been able to do to her in more years than she cared to remember.

The amusement slipped off his face, leaving something altogether more disturbing and intense. Something that, as the old folks liked to say back home, scared the stuffing out of her.

Time to go, Livia.

Pivoting, she walked off toward the house.

The dog scrambled to his feet and ambled along after her.

Chapter 2

Man, what a day.

Hunter Chambers Jr. edged the pickup onto the road and beneath the cool tunnel created by the elms' outstretched branches overhead, heading home after a quick trip to the neighbor's winery. Rolling all the windows down, he enjoyed the rush of air on his overheated face and arms, although the refreshment came at a steep price: now he could smell himself. It wasn't pretty. Atop the mild funk of clean sweat was the not-so-clean aroma of mud. What a winning combination *that* was. It was like he'd rolled several miles in the muck rather than merely walked the vines, picked a few bunches of cabernet—almost ready now; another couple days should do it—and carried the load on his head.

Braking as he went into a switchback, he slid the baseball cap back and swiped his forehead with the back of his hand. Mistake. Big mistake. A glance in the rearview mirror showed an unfortunate brown streak across his skin, adding to the general pigpen effect.

Nasty.

Just the way he liked it.

There was nothing like a hard day outside from dawn to dusk to make him feel like he'd done something, and the sweat and dirt were badges he wore with honor. You couldn't grow grapes sitting nice and clean in the air-conditioned inside—no, siree. Today had been especially productive, especially grueling, and he couldn't be more pleased.

Especially since he'd worked off some of the agitation caused by that woman this morning.

Livia Blake—aka Trouble with a capital *T.*

Having put her out of his mind only through a lot of sweat equity, he wasn't going to think about her now. No, he wasn't. He would keep his mind on, ah…he'd keep his mind on…

Oh, yeah. Shower.

Yeah. An emergency shower was in his immediate future; possibly two. And then it'd be time to open a nice bottle of—

Holy shit.

He came out of the curve and had to cut the wheel hard and stomp the break to keep from plowing into a stupid-ass biker stopped on the shoulder. Hell, it wasn't even the shoulder. Biker and bike were standing on the edge of the road, which was where you hung out when your fondest wish was to be launched three hundred feet into the air and then smashed into roadkill beneath the tires of an oncoming truck.

The biker dropped the bike and jumped aside, way too late, with a shouted "Hey!"

Dumbass. Like he was the reckless one. And Hunter would have been at fault if he'd hit the idiot and culled a weak and clearly stupid member from the herd. Was that fair? Giving the horn a furious honk, he glanced in the side mirror to see if the fool needed help and that was when he realized who it was.

Oh, shit.

It was her. Livia Blake. Trouble.

His gut lurched with a crazy excitement that had nothing to do with playing the Good Samaritan and everything to do with her. *Keep going,* he told himself, but the damn truck was already reversing as though it'd been caught by an invisible tail hook and reeled in. A smarter man would've sent someone back for her, but he and smart hadn't been on speaking terms since he laid eyes on the woman that morning.

Stopping the truck properly on the shoulder, where all stopped vehicles belonged, he got out and took his time about walking back to her. Like the worst kind of Peeping Tom, he sent up a quick prayer of thanksgiving that his shades allowed him to study her with something like discretion. Which was shameful, especially for a man who had a mother and a small daughter. Women were not objects, and they should not be ogled. He was ashamed of himself. Truly. Deep down—deep, deep, *deep* down—in the farthest reaches of his soul, he felt like pond scum for checking her out so thoroughly. God would probably punish him later, and he'd deserve it.

He stared anyway.

That was the funny thing, not that it was really funny. He'd been aware of Livia Blake, of course, and he'd ogled her in the occasional Victoria's Secret catalog that'd strayed across his path over the years. Certainly he'd seen that cover issue of *Sports Illustrated* and lusted, but that was in the generic way that all men universally lusted over all the women in that issue. *Wow. Sexy models…. I wonder what's in the fridge.*

But this…

Seeing her in person was a whole 'nother kettle of fish, and he wasn't quite used to it yet. Especially since she'd far exceeded his expectations and was beautiful in addition to intelligent, funny and intriguing.

Having scrambled back onto the road after darting out of the way, she now bent to pick up the bike. Which was the perfect way for him to appreciate the way her shorts highlighted both her round plum of an ass and her long, smooth and shapely brown legs. This was no tiny little five-footer who you'd be afraid of bending and breaking in bed if things got a little too enthusiastic. Oh, no. This was an Amazon who'd wrap those strong thighs around him—a man, he meant, not *him*—and give as good as she got before demanding more and then more again.

In a fateful move that made this one of the luckiest

days of his life, she'd worn a stretchy little tank top–type thing in white. *White!* Which, out here in the late afternoon sunlight, was really something to see. Maybe that top looked fine in a dressing room, but she'd apparently been riding that bike hard—lucky bike—and she was nice and sweaty. Wet and sweaty. And, as every man in the world knew, white top plus sweaty woman equals a spectacular view of breasts.

No doubt she'd die if she knew it, but he could see… Jesus, he could see everything. Rounded breasts just saggy enough for him to see that they were hers and not some pair purchased via installment plan from a Beverly Hills plastic surgeon. Dark areolae, pointy nipples, the thrilling valley between. Then all that bounty gave way to a narrow waist and curved hips. Anyone who thought all supermodels were bony anorexics with no hips, butt or breasts had never laid eyes on this fantastic creature; no wonder she got millions just for showing up and smiling.

She was one tall drink of water, and he wanted to lower his head and drink.

The face was even better, if that was possible. All the makeup was gone now, not that she'd been wearing much to begin with, replaced with the damp glow of a healthy woman who'd gotten some good exercise. Her hair was up, damp around the edges with curling strands skimming her neck. Those hazel eyes glittered with fire, and her pouty lips were ripe for kissing.

She looked, in short, as though she'd spent a thoroughly satisfying afternoon in bed, and this view of her was definitely not the sort of thing he needed burned into his brain if he wanted to ignore and then forget her.

"You." She kicked the stand down on the mountain bike, hung the helmet from the handlebars, planted her feet wide and jammed her hands on her hips. "I should have known. You're a menace on the road, you know that?"

His blood, he was beginning to discover, flowed a little faster when she was around, and his skin felt a little warmer. It wasn't his imagination and it wasn't just his generalized appreciation of a beautiful woman. There was something about *this* woman that made his heart pound, something intriguing in those bright eyes that he longed to explore.

"I like to drive on the road," he told her. "That's what it's for. Not loitering and admiring the scenery."

"I wasn't admiring the scenery, genius. I have a flat tire."

Yeah, he'd seen that already. He stooped to examine the tire in question, mostly because it brought him much closer to her. Close enough to admire the smoothness of her skin, the attitude in her expression and to smell the clean, earthy musk of her.

Mistake. Big mistake.

And yet, when he stood again, he edged even closer, within kissing distance, if that sort of thing had been on his mind. Only the bike separated them, and God knew they were both tall enough to lean over the bike.

"You and your flat tire should be on the shoulder so you don't get hit."

"That's where we were headed when you and your monster truck almost plowed us down." Here she paused to give him a pointed and disdainful once-over. "What have you been doing, anyway?"

"Working in the fields," he told her, unabashed. No doubt she'd never in her life raised her pretty little manicured hands for anything other than to signal for another glass of champagne. "That's what we do here at the winery."

She wrinkled her nose at him. "Shower much?"

Oh, she was funny. Stripping off his shades so she could see what he was doing, he gave her the kind of look-see she'd just given him, only his was quite a bit more lingering and appreciative. Her cheeks colored accordingly, but she didn't drop that haughty chin by so much as an inch.

"Yeah," he said. "You?"

Giving him a killing glare, she reached for her little pack on the ground and unzipped it. "Thanks for making sure I wasn't killed when I dove out of the way of your speeding death machine. Kindly leave me in peace while I patch this defective Chambers Winery bike tire."

What? Patch? *Her?*

To his astonishment, she withdrew a repair kit and actually looked like she knew what to do with it, which really screwed with his preconceived notions of her as a partying airhead with nothing inside her skull but marshmallow fluff. But, of course, it'd only taken one look into this woman's keen hazel eyes for him to know that there was way more to her than what he could see on the outside.

He'd have to stop misjudging her and give her a chance.

Maybe.

If only he didn't have such fierce reactions to everything about her.

"There's nothing defective at the Chambers Winery, including the bikes. You must have ridden over a nail or something," he informed her gruffly. "And I'll do that for you."

"No, thanks."

"It's the least I can—"

"No, thanks. I can do it."

Yeah, he could see that. The sight of her, tired, dusty, sweaty and proud as she stooped beside the tire, was really doing a number on him. It was a terrible time to discover that he was a caveman at heart, but she shouldn't have to fix that tire, and he was incapable of standing by with his thumb up his ass watching while she did it.

He could do it for her. He wanted to do it for her. An irritating voice inside his head was egging him on, pushing him to prove to her that, even though he wasn't a Hollywood millionaire with flashy cars and a plane, he was strong and capable, and if she needed help while she was here on his land, then he was the one she could rely on.

Crazy, huh?

Insanity. But he still squatted on the other side of that tire, stared at her startled face through the spokes and put his hand on top of hers where it rested on the rubber treads. Something sparked a shiver across his skin. He told himself it was the cooling sweat on his body but that was as blatant a lie as he'd ever told, even to himself. The contact between their flesh tied him up in knots. That, and the wary turbulence in the depths of those astonishing hazel eyes.

"I'll either do this for you or take you back to the bike rental. Your choice, Livia." Her tightening jaw reminded him of his manners. "Please."

"I'm not a spoiled diva."

The stubborn insistence in her voice said it all. She was tired of being stereotyped and dismissed on the basis of her looks, tired of being treated like a china doll that could break and ruin the franchise. She was a strong, capable woman, and she wanted him to see that about her, to acknowledge it.

That pride tugged at his heart. It shouldn't have, but it did.

"I know you're not," he said softly. "And if the truck gets a flat, you can change that for me, okay?"

That got her. A sudden laugh lit up her face and it was every bit as breathtaking as a vivid red sunset on the ocean's horizon or sunlight hitting a rainbow. He started to laugh with her, but halfway through the maneuver his throat seized up and he could only stare, wishing she'd release him from whatever spell she'd spun around him.

"You're just being nice because you know I'm going to try and get you fired."

He floundered, trying to get his voice back online. He wasn't quite sure why he hadn't told her that he was one of the Chambers that owned the winery, or why he'd given her his old nickname, J.R. for junior, rather than his real name, other than the idea of her trying to get his parents to fire him was hilarious.

This woman…she did things to him.

"Can we go now?"

"Yeah." Her smile faded, probably because she'd seen—she had to see—how she intrigued him, how he wanted her. There were lots of things he was good at, but controlling his reactions to her didn't seem to be one of them. Their touching hands became a fulcrum, the ground zero of a growing wave of heat that would ignite a fire capable of torching all these surrounding elms if they weren't careful. "Can I have my hand back now?"

"Yeah," he said, meaning it, and his brain sent the command to his hand: *let go.*

It took three or four beats after that for his hand to obey.

He stood, flustered, and she stood, clearing her throat. They didn't look at each other. This unspoken signal made them look in other directions while he loaded the bike in the truck's bed and she gathered up the helmet and her pack. They got in and he started the engine. No eye contact. They buckled up, staring out of their respective windows.

It didn't matter. The damage had already been done and the air between them vibrated and sizzled accordingly, reminding him of the crackling energy created by the light sabers in the *Star Wars* movies. Which wasn't a good sign.

He put the truck in gear and gripped the wheel with palms that were now wet like the rest of him but for an entirely different reason.

Drive, man. Keep your trap shut and drive. The sooner she's out of your truck, the better.

Don't say anything stupid.

"Livia?"

There was all kinds of yearning in his hoarse voice but it didn't seem to reach her. She kept her head resolutely turned toward her window and didn't answer.

"Are we developing a problem here?"

"No," she said flatly.

Right.

Recognizing the lie for what it was, he drove off toward the winery.

Okay, girl, Livia told herself. *Okay. This is not a big deal. There're only a few miles to go back to the winery and you'll be safe there. Not that you're in danger or anything.* Physical danger, that was. *Just ignore the sexy man because you're not here in Napa for a hookup or any other kind of romantic adventure. Stare out your window and think about what you need to pack for the shoot in Mexico at the end of the month.*

She thought hard, possibly damaging her discombobulated brain in the process.

What did she need? Mexico was hot, right, so she'd need—what?

Oh, wait. *Sunscreen.* Good! Good start! Great job ignoring the sexy man!

Yes. She could do this. She'd need sunscreen, and she'd also need—

"Are you cold?" he asked, adjusting the vents.

Damn. Was he doing that on purpose or what? Was his voice always this velvety rasp that crept its way under her skin—when he wasn't barking at her, that was? And why was he being so thoughtful and considerate all of the sudden when she knew darn well he'd already written her off as a Tinseltown flake with a worthless job flashing pretty smiles at the cameras for big money?

Why did his presence tie her belly up in crazy little knots?

He was dirty like a field hand, for God's sake! Dirty, grouchy and arrogant. What was so thrilling about that? True, he wore a Negro League baseball cap—the black background with red lettering of the Indianapolis Clowns—so he couldn't be all bad, but he was definitely mostly bad. So why was he making her unravel like a ninth-grader crushing on the prom king? Why did the musky scent of him and the indecipherable light in his golden eyes turn her into a quivering pool of mush?

At least he'd stopped touching her. Thank goodness for small favors.

"Ah, no," she said, clearing her throat. "Thanks."

They rode in silence for a way, which was good. Using the least amount of words possible seemed to be his thing, so as long as she kept quiet and didn't babble or engage him in any way, this whole disconcerting interlude between them could pass without further incident.

Nice. She had a workable plan.

"What exactly do you do at the winery?" she asked.

He hesitated, keeping his eyes on the road. "I grow the grapes. And I make the wine."

A lightbulb went off over her head. She'd known this guy was way too intelligent to dig irrigation ditches or some such all day, despite his appearance.

"Oh. So you're a viticulturist and enologist?"

His jaw hit his lap with surprise and he glanced over, all wide-eyed astonishment. "Yeah."

Annoyance warred with dark triumph inside her gut. So he was surprised she knew a couple multisyllable words, was he? Did he think she was too dumb and clueless to do a little reading about a vineyard before she showed up at one? Bozo.

"Keep your eyes on the road, please," she snapped. "I don't know why you're so determined to kill me with this truck."

He jerked his gaze back to the road. "Sorry. Not many people know the words."

"Well, I'm not like many people, am I?" She didn't

bother keeping the ice out of her voice; she wasn't ready to accept his apology just yet.

"No." A muscle ticked in the back of his jaw. "You sure as hell aren't."

"So you're a scientist. Did you go to UC Davis? I know they've got a program there—"

"No." The edge of his lip curled, as though he was fighting a smile. "I went to Washington State."

"So how long have you been working here?"

He paused. "Long time."

"Do you like it?"

"Yeah."

"Is it true that you can tell when the grapes are ripe by squeezing them and seeing if the juice makes a little star-shaped pattern?"

His brows crept toward his hairline. They drove a good several hundred feet before he answered, "Yep."

Irritated all over again, she glared at the side of his face. "Feel free to jump in anytime and tell me some fun facts about making wine. Maybe we could carry on a conversation."

"I doubt there's anything I could say that you don't already know."

"What a great ambassador for the Chambers Winery you are," she muttered. "I can hardly wait to go back home and give this place a one-star rating on all the review sites."

They rolled up to a stop sign just then and he took the opportunity to stare into her eyes with what seemed like bewilderment and sincerity. "Livia," he said tiredly, "at this point, I'm just trying to keep my head from exploding off my shoulders."

Well, what the hell was that supposed to mean? Was that an insult? A compliment?

Stymied, she snapped her mouth shut, crossed her arms over her chest and kept her head turned toward the window. See? She knew she should've kept her mouth shut. Why'd she let her weird fascination with this guy overwhelm her good sense? They were oil and water, in case she still hadn't gotten it through her thick head, and any conversation between them was impossible, notwithstanding all her best intentions.

Luckily, they'd arrived. Driving past the tasteful stone sign that read Chambers Winery, he pulled up to the crowded bike rental stand and put the car in Park.

"Thanks for the ride," she snapped. Desperate to get out of his truck and be done with him, forever, she snatched her pack off the floor and reached for the door handle. "I can get the bike myself—"

"Here." Something soft tapped her on the arm and she looked over her shoulder to discover that he'd produced a clean powder-blue Chambers Winery T-shirt from somewhere. "Put this on."

"I don't need it."

"You're cold," he insisted.

Cold? Did he not see her sweat-slicked face? "Are you crazy?" she began, but then he gave her chest a pointed once-over and she glanced down with dawning understanding.

Oh, God. Everything—everything!—was on display

down there; she might as well have photographed her girls and posted them on the nearest billboard. Cheeks burning with humiliation, she snatched the shirt and jerked it on, taking two attempts to get her right arm into its sleeve.

"You could have mentioned that earlier," she snarled when her head emerged.

He shrugged. "I couldn't resist the view."

Would it be wrong to scratch his eyes out? The local police would understand given the circumstances, right? And why did she *still* feel this strong connection to him and, worse, the driving need to understand what went on behind the honey-colored crystal of his eyes?

"I can't get a read on you." It wasn't the wisest confession she'd ever made but she couldn't hold it back. "I can't figure out if you're the world's biggest jerk or a great guy."

Renewed heat swallowed up his amusement and that smirk disappeared, giving way to naked intensity that had her belly fluttering and her toes curling.

"Does it matter to you which one I am, Sweet Livie?"

"No," she lied. "It doesn't matter to me at all."

Chapter 3

Livia tiptoed through the small foyer and inched the door of her guesthouse open just enough to let in a sliver of early morning sunshine. Peering out, she saw, to her delight, that the heavy mist seemed to have burned off since she woke from a near-dead sleep forty-five minutes ago (something about this wonderful mountain air really did it for her), and it looked like it'd be a great day for—

Bark!

Aaaannnd he was still there.

Resigned to her fate, she sighed, gave up her covert routine and stepped out onto the porch, where Marmaduke had taken up residence on one of her Adirondack chairs. Had he slept there last night, keeping a sweet but misguided watch over her little temporary home? She was beginning to think he had. He'd definitely been guarding his post when room service arrived with her breakfast oatmeal, granola and fruit earlier. Clearly she shouldn't have slipped him that tiny piece of banana; she could see that now. It'd only encouraged him, and the Dog Wrangler wouldn't approve of a dog being fed people food. Now she was apparently stuck with the monster.

Served her right for being softhearted.

The dog, sensing weakness, cocked his enormous head, regarded her with those melted chocolate eyes and managed to look less goofy and more cute.

"Hello, poochie," she murmured, scratching his ears again and wishing she knew his name. His tail wagged, thumping the chair hard enough to cause splinters in the wood. "Are you trying to get more banan-aaa? Well, I don't have any. I don't have annn-yyy."

The dog showed every indication of forgiving her. He gave her hand a sweeping lick with a tongue the size of a slab of beef and lurched to his feet, tail swinging and ready to begin a full day of following her around.

Right.

First thing on her agenda: complaining to the owners about J.R.

The main house was a hive of activity with people converging around bicycles lined up on the cobblestone courtyard beyond the huge front porch. This must be the daily tour she'd read about in the brochure; she'd have to sign up for the one tomorrow. Riding down these country roads through the swaying vines and past the river sounded like heaven to her, and the tour ended with a winery tour and tasting. Who could turn that down?

Skirting the friendly crowd, several of whom smiled at her with respectful recognition but showed no signs of wanting an autograph or picture with her, thank goodness, she and her four-legged shadow entered the huge main lobby.

It was incredibly beautiful in that Western open-sky kind of way. Huge windows, vaulted ceiling, an enormous stone hearth with a roaring fire to ward off the morning's chill. Seating areas with leather sofas and chairs invited people to sit, stay awhile and visit and the hearty scent of good brew wafting from the fully stocked coffee bar in the corner invited her to never leave. Ever.

Another cup of coffee was just the thing she needed before—

Wait. Was that the little girl again, over there peering at her from behind the grand piano? It was. Crouched down with only her face visible around the gleaming ebony bench, she was all wide-eyed interest and quivering excitement.

Livia smiled and waved.

The girl giggled, clapped her hand over her mouth and disappeared into the shadows.

Livia laughed. She'd gotten a giggle out of her little stalker this time, so that was progress, right?

Helping herself to a huge powder-blue Chambers Winery mug, she filled it with her morning drink, which was essentially a cup of milk with just enough coffee in it to turn it tan. No nasty skim milk for her today, thanks. On this vacation, she was going to eat and drink to her heart's content, and that meant—oh, wow, look at the creamy deliciousness!—whole milk.

Taking a sip, she moaned in ecstasy. The dog, who was nothing but a blatant opportunist, whined with hope.

"None for you," she said sharply.

He whined again, ears drooping.

"Okay," she muttered to herself, glancing at all the blue-shirted employees for the one she wanted. Time to talk to...oh, there she was at the reception counter. She recognized her from her photo on the winery's Web site. "Excuse me. Are you Mrs. Chambers?"

The older woman, who'd been typing something into the computer, looked up and smiled. "I certainly am. So if you love it here and you're having the time of your life, you have me to thank. But if you're having any sort of problem with the food or service or anything, it's my husband's fault and I had nothing to do with it. You can blame him."

Laughing, Livia stuck out her hand. "I'm Livia Blake. I'm great friends with Rachel Wellesley. You've got a fantastic place here."

"Well, any friend of my son Ethan's fiancée is practically family. It's so nice to meet you." Mrs. Chambers was lovely, with salt-and-pepper natural waves and happy eyes that crinkled at the corners. She had a warm, double-handed grip and wide smile that made Livia feel like a long-lost niece or something. "Your pictures don't do you justice."

Livia flushed. "Thank you so much."

"I see you've met Willard."

"Willard." The dog, hearing his name, perked up and waited at attention. "So that's his name. Wait—*Willard?*"

"Don't blame me," Mrs. Chambers said. "My granddaughter named him. He's not bothering you, is he? We're still trying to civilize him. He's a stray."

Willard, the manipulator, chose that exact moment to rub his big fat head against Livia's leg, leaving a splotch of saliva on her cargo pants. What could she do but give him a nice scratch under his collar?

"Oh, he's fine," Livia said. "I'm used to him now."

"Well, you let me know if he doesn't behave."

"Actually, there's someone else here who isn't behaving—"

"Oh, no."

"—J.R.? One of your employees?"

Mrs. Chambers gaped at her. "J.R.?"

Livia hated to sound like a tattletale, but she wasn't going to pull her punches. "He was very rude to me when I arrived yesterday. I thought you should know."

"*J.R.?*"

"Yes, and he said you'd had problems with him before. So, I just—with a bed-and-breakfast this lovely, I thought you probably didn't want employees giving paying guests a hard time. Maybe you'll want to speak to him about that."

A sudden speculative gleam sparked to life in Mrs. Chamber's eye, almost as though she knew Mr. Arrogant had made Livia's belly flutter with unmentionable desires. It figured. A man like that—all muscles, dimples, testosterone and bad attitude—was nothing but trouble to any nearby female guests, a fact of which Mrs. Chambers was probably well aware.

Sure enough. "I certainly will talk to J.R. and get to the bottom of this right away," Mrs. Chambers said. "Don't you worry."

"I don't want to get him fired or anything," Livia said quickly.

"I understand." Mrs. Chambers looked utterly sincere but Livia couldn't shake the feeling that there was a teensy bit of amusement in there somewhere, and she didn't get it. "You leave him to me."

"Well." Livia hesitated. Was there some punch line she was missing here? "Thank you."

"Have a lovely day, dear. Feel free to explore."

"I will." Livia drifted away, with nowhere in particular to go.

O-kaaay.

Now that her complaint was officially lodged, it was time to dooo...

Nothing. Absolutely nothing. Yay!

The light and easy feeling of being an eagle, soaring high and free, was so overwhelming she had to sit in one of the cozy chairs before the fire and let it sink in while she sipped her coffee. For once she didn't have to check her watch every three minutes and then dash off to a flight or a shoot. For once she didn't need to have the cell phone glued to her ear and take every urgent call that came through from her agent, manager or personal assistant. For once she could sit on her bee-hind and be as lazy as she wanted.

Feeling ridiculous and happy, she grinned down at Willard, who'd collapsed atop her feet for an impromptu rest. Ever watchful, he peered up at her, brows raised, and lounged patiently while she finished her drink. Yawning with a startling display of sharp white teeth, he waited for his marching orders.

"All right, you big oaf. If you'll get off me, we can get going."

Apparently the dog spoke a little English. After another jaw-cracking yawn and stretch, he heaved himself upright—what'd this beast weigh, anyway? One-eighty? Two hundred?—and trotted over to a back door, which seemed as good a place to start as any.

Out they went. It hadn't warmed up much but the bright sun had burned off the last of the mist and it was already a gorgeous day. She wandered past the open-air restaurant with its green market umbrellas and enormous trellis twined with wisteria vines thicker than her arms and paused on a stone terrace overlooking the rolling hills and the grapes.

Leaning her elbows on the thick stone wall, she breathed in the sweet air, which was so different from the low-hanging and unidentifiable gray cloud that smothered L.A. and the exhaust-filled fumes of New

York. It was so clean and pure she was surprised her lungs didn't seize up in shock.

In the far distance she could see workers walking between the rows, probably assessing the grapes for ripeness. It was, she knew from her pretrip research, almost harvest time. Maybe she could even pick a grape or two before her trip was over.

Pulling out her 35mm camera, which she'd slung over her shoulder earlier, she took a few shots. Maybe she could start a Napa Valley scrapbook. She did love scrapbooking. Willard obligingly posed for a couple of pictures and then they were off again, wandering with nowhere to be.

Wasn't there a heated pool around here somewhere? And a spa? Wait…yeah. Over there. Inside an enormous wrought-iron fence was one of those deep blue natural pools that looked like a pond carved out of a hill. There was even a stone waterfall, as though they'd stumbled into some sort of hidden jungle oasis. People lounged on towel-covered chairs beneath market umbrellas, chatting happily and sipping wine from oversized glasses.

Livia focused her lens, snapping a few more shots and wishing she could stay here in this laid-back and peaceful environment forever, or at least discover somewhere in L.A. that made her feel this mellow.

"Not swimming?"

So much for relaxation. J.R.'s deep voice way too close to her ear wound her up tight, making her skin tingle and her breath come short. Resolutely determined to ignore him, she kept her elbows on the fence and the camera up to her face, taking pictures of God knew what in her sudden distraction—probably scattered flip-flops, empty orange juice glasses and the corners of peoples' noses. He didn't take the hint. Big surprise. Doing the worst possible thing, he rested his elbow on the fence beside hers, igniting her skin with the slight brush of his.

God.

"Hello, J.R.," she finally said, keeping her voice tart and refusing to look at him. "Stalking me again?"

Too bad the smug amusement in his voice disturbed her as much as his touch and masculinity. "Actually, I've been staking out the pool. I don't want to miss it if you take a dip. Will you be putting on a two-piece anytime soon?"

That did it. Jerking the camera down, she glared at him, meeting that honey gaze and feeling its kick right in her solar plexus. He wore the Chambers Winery colors and a Negro League cap again today, but he was fresh and clean, smelling of soap and masculine deliciousness. The lethal combination of his arrogance, proximity and boyish wickedness—he had dimples! *Dimples!*—was making her agitated and hot enough to burst out of her sensitized skin, and it really pissed her off.

"I spoke to Mrs. Chambers about you a little while ago. You should probably update your résumé."

He laughed and that was sexy, too. "Thanks for the warning. So you like being on the other side of the lens, eh?"

"Yes. Not that it's any of your business."

"Are you any good?"

"Naturally," she said, hoping he didn't ask to see any of her last few shots. "Don't you have some work to do in the fields? Mud to wallow in? Something?"

He tsked. "If you're not nice to me, Livia, I'm not going to give you your present."

Present? Really? That sounded interesting, but she couldn't be swayed from her absolute and unadulterated dislike of him. This man disturbed her way too much. "Thanks, but I don't want anything from you. Except maybe your swift departure."

"Really?" That amber gaze skimmed over her, silky-smooth and smoldering. "You sure about that?" he wondered softly.

She stared at him, her dry mouth and tight throat rendering her incapable of answering. That was bad enough. Worse was the sudden fullness in her breasts and the subtle but insistent ache between her thighs.

The moment lasted way too long, until she managed to find her voice and create a diversion. "I wouldn't mind taking your Black Yankees cap."

His eyes widened with surprise. "You know the Negro Leagues?"

"I...love baseball. I'm reading a Jackie Robinson biography right now."

"Oh," he said faintly.

So much for her diversion. This revelation that they had baseball in common seemed only to sharpen his interest; she felt it swirling around her and wrapping her up tight in its cocoon.

He didn't seem to like it any better than she did and his next words came with great reluctance, as though he was kicking them out of his mouth.

"You're really something. You know that?"

She couldn't answer. The air was pregnant with so many things between them that she couldn't trust her voice.

He blinked and recovered and, unsmiling, presented her with a bowl that he'd hidden behind his back.

Oh, wow. It was filled with the most beautiful dusty purple grapes.

"Oh," she said helplessly, feeling special and decadent, like a latter-day Cleopatra who'd been gifted with all the treasures this wondrous land had to offer. "Thank you."

He dimpled again, but the piercing intensity with which he studied her didn't diminish by so much as a watt. Was this a seduction? Did he know that she would have thrown a diamond bracelet back in his face, but her driving curiosity would never let her reject a bowl of grapes from a vintner?

"You're welcome. They're pinot noir. Do you drink pinot?"

"Yes. Are they ripe?"

They had to be; she could smell their fragrance already.

"You tell me."

He pulled one off the stem for her and her unwilling gaze went to his hands, which were long-fingered and even with short, clean nails. That hand had touched hers yesterday. That hand had made her feel all kinds of unwanted sensations. That hand was trouble.

To her agonized dismay, he wiped and then squeezed the grape in a careful grip between thumb and forefinger, making her wonder how a man this size could be so gentle. The grape burst open into a star pattern with a bead of dark juice that was one of the most sensual things she'd ever seen as it trickled down his brown skin.

Her gaze flickered up to his face. She couldn't breathe. "It's ripe."

"What does it taste like?"

He held it to her lips, utterly still and watchful, as though the earth would stop revolving for him until he saw what she would do. There was only one thing she could do. Opening her mouth, she took the grape, taking care to brush his thumb with her tongue as she did.

His breath hitched. "What does it taste like?"

His skin tasted salty and warm, absolutely delicious. But he was probably asking about the grape, so she pressed it to the roof of her mouth, crushing it and letting the flavors wash over her. "I don't know—"

"Yes, you do," he urged.

She thought hard, struggling to put it into words. "Strawberry, maybe…or is it raspberry? With something that's a little, I don't know…a little spicy."

That pleased him. Those eyes of his crinkled at the corners, thrilling her beyond all reason. "I'll make a world-class viticulturist out of you yet, Livia," he murmured.

With that, he pressed the bowl into her hands and turned to go, granting her wish to be alone, and she stared after him, wanting him to stay.

Chapter 4

The next day, after a bicycle tour in the morning and an open-air lunch on the terrace, Livia resumed her exploration of the winery grounds. She still hadn't seen the stone chapel that was around here somewhere—the whole point of her visit was to scope out the chapel and report back to Rachel on its suitability for her wedding— and there was no time like the present to find it.

There'd been no sign of J.R., and she was glad about that.

Really. She was glad.

"Come on, Willard." Heading to the far end of the terrace, she consulted her map and clicked her fingers at her sidekick, who'd again been outside her door this morning and had waited for her at the bike stand during the tour.

No answer.

"Willard?" She raised her head and looked around. Nothing.

Had that silly dog finally abandoned her? Feeling unaccountably disgruntled, she put her hands on her hips and scanned in all directions for her unfaithful companion, but there was no sign of him.

Well, fine, Willard. *Fine.* She could explore by her damn self.

At the edge of the terrace, though, she discovered a surprise. A pretty little rock waterfall had been carved into the hill like stair steps and the water flowed into a small pond with the kind of relaxing trickle that people back in L.A. acquired through the use of programmable sleep machines available in high-end gadget stores. Potted plants, flowers and lush grass surrounded the whole area, and there, at the end of several enormous stepping stones, sat the biggest doghouse Livia had ever seen. At least she thought it was a doghouse.

Wait—was it a doghouse?

Fire-engine red with a black roof and honest-to-God wraparound porch with white rails, it had a white bone-shaped cutout over the arched doorway, so…yeah, it was definitely a doghouse. Oh, and there behind it were King Kong–sized stainless steel food and water bowls, so—

"Are you a princess?"

Whoa. Unidentified small person voice. Was this the girl that'd been following her? Livia glanced all around but there was no one in sight. "Uh," she said, still searching and beginning to feel dumb, "are you talking to me?"

"Yes."

"Where are you?"

"Here."

That time she got a bead on the voice. It came from the general direction of the doghouse…. There it was! A flash of movement inside the house and the unmistakable glint of a pair of large eyes that did not belong to Willard.

Creeping closer, Livia squatted and squinted into the dark depths of the house. At the same time, a flashlight clicked on, settled under a small chin and illuminated a girl's face—it was her shy little friend—with the eerie up-lighting usually seen only in horror movies and at sleepovers.

Deeper into the doghouse—geez, how much square footage did this thing have?—lounged Willard, chomping on a chew toy of some kind. In front of the girl was a collection of lunging and snarling plastic dinosaurs and dragons that overflowed from their plastic bin.

"Hi," Livia said.

The girl regarded her solemnly, the effect intensified by the flashlight's glow, and spoke in a Vincent Price–like, creepy voice. "You may enter the dragon's den if you utter the secret password."

"Ah," Livia said, not at all certain she wanted to fold her body up in there with that dog, no matter how much space there was. "I don't think I know the secret pass—"

"Guess."

"Ah. Okay. Hmm. Is it *please?* No, that'd be dumb. *Princess? Pterodactyl?*"

"It's pteranodon."

"Sorry. I knew that. Pteranodon?"

"No."

"Umm… Belle? Aurora? Snow White? Mulan? Pocahontas?"

The girl took mercy on Livia and apparently decided she'd made enough of an effort, which was good because Livia's knees were beginning to creak.

"The password is *Tiana*. You may enter."

Livia was afraid of that. "Tell you what. Why don't I just sit right here and—"

"Enter," the girl commanded in that ghostly voice.

"Enter. Right."

What else could she do but drop to all fours and crawl into the doghouse? She sincerely hoped that there were no paparazzi loitering nearby in the bushes. The cover shot on the week's tabloids would include a close-up picture of her butt, which would look like a double-wide trailer, and the headline would read something along the lines of "Guess Which Supermodel is Losing the Battle with Cellulite?"

Nice.

To her immense surprise and relief, though, once she got through the cramped opening the house was quite spacious. More like a dog mansion. Willard seemed happy to be reunited with her and, when she sat cross-legged, put his head in her lap.

Thus settled, she turned to the girl. "What's your name?"

"You may only speak when you have the light of truth."

"Oh. Sorry." Livia accepted the flashlight and turned it on to her own face, trying to match the girl's somber tone. "What is thy name, little girl?"

The girl giggled, revealing half an adult-sized tooth, a gap and what seemed like several dozen pearl-sized baby teeth, but didn't answer until she'd taken the flashlight back.

"My name is Kendra Chambers." Aha. This must be Mrs. Chambers's granddaughter, the one they all had to thank for christening Willard. "What is thy name and is thy—?"

"Art thou," Livia corrected.

"Art thou a princess?"

Another flashlight switch. "Livia Blake is my name. I am no princess, fair maiden, alas. My parents were neither king nor queen."

"Alas," Kendra agreed solemnly.

They stared at each other for one long beat and then burst into laughter. The girl was adorable, with that perfectly smooth, beautiful baby skin that most women in L.A. achieved only through Botox, dimples, eyes of an indeterminate dark color and bouncing curly twists that reached her shoulders.

"What're you doing in here, you silly girl?" Livia asked, dropping the spooky voice and flashlight routine. "Don't you know this is a doghouse?"

"Willard doesn't mind sharing."

"Oh, yeah? Well, where's your mommy? Who's watching you right now in case Willard wants to eat you for lunch?"

Oh, no. That was clearly the wrong thing to ask because the girl's sweet little smile slipped away, leaving her forlorn and lost. Still, she blinked back her tears in a stunning stab at bravery. "Mommy died three years ago."

"Oh, no."

"When I was three."

"I'm so sorry." Livia touched the girl's soft chin and then decided that more silliness was required. "So if that was three years ago, then that makes you, what—sixteen right now?"

"Nooo!"

"Seventeen?"

"I'm six! *Six!* And three-quarters."

"Wow. I thought you were a teenager for sure." Grinning, Livia pointed to the dinosaur display. "What's all this?"

Kendra perked right up again and reached for that favorite prehistoric beast of kids the world over: a T. rex. "This is a Tyrannosaurus rex. *Rex* means king because he was the king of the dinosaurs and usually ate everyone else. This one's a brachiosaurus, and he was really tall— see his neck?—but he only ate plants and stuff. And this one…"

There was more, but Livia was too busy staring at this adorable chattering child to absorb it. What a precious angel, so smart and strong, so funny and interesting. Guided by some long-dormant mothering instinct that overrode social niceties like, say, not touching kids who didn't belong to you, she reached out and stroked Kendra's cheek, which was the finest caramel velvet. Then, when Kendra kept on yakking and didn't miss a single beat in her dino lecture, Livia smoothed one of the girl's bouncing spiral twists. The satiny feel of it between her fingers was more wondrous than that of any of the five-figure couture gowns she'd worn over the years.

An ache of longing gripped her around the throat and settled in her chest.

Beautiful little girl.

"Which one do you like?" Kendra was asking.

"I don't know." Trying to get back in the game, Livia sifted through the plastic, looking for her favorite. "Do you have one of those—I can't think of the name, but they're the ones with the scary long claws that hunt in a pack."

"Velociraptor?"

"Yeah. Velociraptor."

"Here it is!" Brimming with triumph, Kendra located the model in question and handed it to Livia. "Did you know these guys were related to birds?"

"No way."

"Yuh-huh. And some of them maybe had feathers."

"Get outta here."

Nodding vigorously, Kendra scootched around, scrambled out of the doghouse and held out a tiny hand with sparkly purple nail polish to help Livia up and out. "I'll show you! It's in my book in my room. They have drawings, too, so you can see."

Oh, thank goodness. Another minute sitting on the ground like this would make her butt go numb and her hips and knees seize up. Unfolding her long limbs, Livia was in an undignified crawling crouch, half in and half out of the doghouse, and had just reached for Kendra's hand when that familiar male voice, acid once again with disapproval, boomed over her.

"What did you do to my daughter?"

Hunter stared at the scene in front of him, wondering when he'd slipped through the rabbit hole and into Wonderland with Alice. Or maybe he'd plunged into the twilight zone or been out in the fields too long this morning with the bright sun beating down on his unprotected head. Possibly he was just insane.

Whatever.

The bottom line was he couldn't believe his freaking eyes.

Because there, emerging from the doghouse, was Livia, the woman who'd become his recent obsession even though he'd spent the last day or so trying to avoid her. Livia, a supermodel who, if *Forbes* could be believed, had made about, oh, forty million last year, give or take—an intelligent and intriguing beauty so statuesque and stunning she was as fantastic and unreal as a unicorn sitting next to the pot of gold at the end of the rainbow.

Livia. In the doghouse. With his daughter and her goofy dog Willard.

And here's where it got weird.

Kendra was talking to her. Kendra, the girl who'd been so severely traumatized by her mother's death in a car accident three years ago that she'd lost most of her words at age three, scaring the whole family to death. Kendra, who shut down in new situations with new people.

Kendra "The Silent" was talking. Livia Blake had, in a few short minutes, achieved a breakthrough with his child that was nothing short of a miracle.

Holy shit.

"What did you do to my daughter?"

Finished straightening and smoothing her clothes, Livia scowled at him, her hazel cat eyes narrowed into a killing glare. "I didn't do anything to her, just like I didn't do anything to your dog the other day. Why are you always accusing me of wrongdoing? We were talking and playing. She showed me her dinosaurs. No harm done."

Brilliant, Chambers. Way to bark at the pretty lady and piss her off. Again. You should try to bottle that charm and sell it. Eau de Knucklehead. You could make a fortune.

"I didn't mean—"

"Save it." Though clearly angry, she dialed it all back and stooped to face Kendra with a smile. "Thanks for letting me into the dragon's den, sweetie. I'll see you later."

"No!" Kendra grabbed Livia's hand and whirled on him with a healthy dose of six-year-old ferocity. "Livia's going to—"

"*Miss* Livia," he corrected.

Now hopping from one foot to the other, Kendra amped up her plea. "Miss Livia's going to come see my dinosaur books because she doesn't believe dinosaurs are related to birds. O-kaaay? Please? Please, please, please?"

"That's okay," Livia told Kendra. "We'll do it another—"

"Actually, we'd love to have you come for dinner," he said.

Livia gaped at him, probably because he'd crossed over the line they'd been skirting. Flirting was one thing. An attraction—and Lord knew they had an attraction going here—didn't have to lead to anything. But if they spent time together, then they'd start down a road that inevitably led to them sleeping together and who knew what after that.

It was a bad idea; he understood that. Their different worlds had collided for only a few days while she was here in Napa, pretty much as if a zebra had taken a submarine into the Caribbean and taken up with a dolphin, but what could he do? Ignore the power of his infatuation with this one special woman who was good with dogs and children, loved baseball, had a nose for grapes *and* was sexy as hell?

No.

If he'd ever had a choice about it, he didn't now. If he

didn't at least try to get to know her better, regret would haunt his steps for a good long time.

Livia still hadn't recovered from her surprise, so he took advantage of the momentary silence to send Kendra on her way. He had no idea what he thought he'd say or do next, only that it involved him and Livia alone. "Go on up to the house, Dino-Girl. Grandma's looking for you."

Kendra didn't want to go. "But Miss Livia—"

"I'll see if she wants to come to dinner. So tell her you'll see her later."

Being no dummy, Kendra whirled on Livia and turned on the charm. "Please will you come to dinner? Pleeeeaaaaase?"

There were many advantages to having the world's cutest kid and he was witnessing one of them right now: people couldn't say no to her. It made his life tough when she turned those big baby browns on him and he had to be the bad guy, but right now he thought his daughter was pretty spectacular. Hell, he ought to buy her another dino figure later as a reward.

Livia's uncertain gaze wavered between the two of them, and then she caved. "I'd love to come to dinner. See you later, okay?"

"Yay," Kendra sang, already hopping down the path. "Bye!"

"Bye," they called.

Then the girl disappeared, leaving awkward silence behind.

It didn't take Livia long to fill it with an accusation. "You're Hunter *Chambers*."

"Right."

"How the hell do you get J.R. out of Hunter? A typo on your birth certificate?"

"It's for junior. My dad is senior."

"Your family owns this vineyard."

"Right."

"So you're not some random employee that I could get into trouble or fired say by complaining to your mother, are you?"

"Nope."

Her kissable lips flattened into a sexy little pout and her faint drawl intensified. "So you had a nice laugh at my expense."

"I sure did." Matter of fact, he was having a hard time not laughing now but, judging by the steely flash in her eyes, she wasn't above taking a swing at him, so he kept his current amusement to himself.

"Have I offended you in some way?" she asked sharply.

"No."

"Because you've had an issue with me since the second I got here. First you accuse me of doing something to your dog, and then you accuse…"

There was a whole lot more in that vein, but his mind wandered.

They were attracted to each other, he and Livia Blake, supermodel. When they were near each other, they all but ignited the air between them. Maybe she wished she didn't feel it, but he could see it in her overbright eyes and flushed cheeks, and he'd definitely felt it when she licked that grape juice off his thumb.

"...and we were just sitting there! In broad daylight, looking at dinosaurs! Is that a crime now? What did..."

It'd been a long time since he'd had anything other than the occasional booty call with a woman, and an even longer time since he'd felt this fascinated by anyone, this enthralled.

"...I am a nice person! I don't care what you may have heard about me on *Entertainment Tonight* or some other show. And I don't appreciate..."

She wasn't for him. A woman like this could snap her fingers and have any man she wanted, from European royalty to billionaires, from professional athletes to U.S. senators, and he was only fooling himself if he thought he was anything other than a farmer. A grape farmer, true, with one of the best labels in Napa, but still just a farmer. Phylloxera could attack the roots of his vines tomorrow, the crops would be ruined and he'd be in a world of hurt. He was doing pretty well for himself, but there was no danger of him being able to afford his own plane anytime soon.

"...what happened to the benefit of the doubt? Or doesn't that apply here in northern California? Do I have horns on my head? Is that it?"

Still.

He wasn't a bad guy even if he wasn't rich and famous, and she, when it was all said and done, was just a woman. He was here now, and she was here now. They were attracted to each other and that was pretty basic no matter how you sliced it. And he really, really wanted to get to know her.

Great. Decision made. He tuned back in to her rant.

"...think you owe me an apology?"

Oh, man. He liked this one. A lot. All attitude with just enough sweetness thrown in to make him sweat. He'd bet she had those hands on her hips again and—yep. There they were.

"Hello-ooo! I am talking to you—"

"Livia, do me a favor and shut up a minute so I can kiss you, okay?"

The second her mouth popped open in surprise, he made his move. No point in giving her time to protest or manufacture more denials about being interested in him. Cupping her face between his hands—Christ, when had he ever felt something so soft and fine?—he leaned in to taste her.

Chapter 5

He'd meant it to be an easy brush of lips, a nibble at most. A quick, simple and nonverbal statement of intent—assuming, of course, that she didn't smack him away. But then they were connected and she made one of those sounds that women do. It was a coo, raw and sexual, and it sent him over an edge he hadn't even known was there. He pulled back, shaken and burned, and stared at her. *Livia.* She was all shocked, wide eyes, heaving breasts and wet lips, and he wanted her.

He *wanted* her.

Tightening his grip into her nape, he pulled her in again, devouring her this time without any need or ability to be gentle. She made it easy for him, opening her sweet mouth and slipping her tongue into his. *God.* This woman did something dangerous to him, and he was so far gone he couldn't expose his jugular fast enough.

Someone moaned; it was impossible to tell who because there was no separation between them, nothing but a perfect, seamless whole. And when he found himself delving into her hair, caressing her back and reaching for her ass to press her writhing hips against his, he let her go because the time wasn't right.

But, he now knew, the time would definitely come.

The sound of their mutual panting filled the space until he could talk again.

"Thanks for your help with Kendra. You're really good with her."

She'd backed up a step and put her fingers to her lips. Now she blinked off some of her sensual daze and studied him with a keen focus. "I wasn't helping her. I was enjoying her. Why wouldn't I? She's a bright, beautiful child."

"A bright, beautiful child who never talks to strangers and has a tough time coming out of her shell."

"She wouldn't stop talking."

"I know," he said. "That's not normal for her. Ever since my wife died—"

"Oh." Something in her expression darkened, closing off from him and shutting him out in the cold. He didn't like it in the cold. "So that's what that was? A gratitude kiss?"

Is that what she thought? Was she insane? "No, but I'm happy to give you a gratitude kiss if you're in the mood."

"What was that then?"

Some questions didn't need answering, so he simply stared at her until a knowing flush crept over her face and that glittering light behind her eyes came back on again.

"You know what that was, Livia," he said softly.

She met his gaze, not quite smiling but not looking away, either.

Taking that as agreement, he leaned in for another kiss, a quick one this time, because he was already addicted and he couldn't help himself. Just that simple touch made her sigh and soften, and he realized she couldn't help herself either.

This was dangerous, what they were doing.

And he couldn't hurtle toward it fast enough.

"Dinner's at six-thirty," he told her. "I'll be waiting for you."

Hunter watched Livia go and barely resisted the overwhelming urge to call her back. What the hell was wrong with him? You'd think she was departing for a one-way trip to a neighboring universe, forever taking the secrets to food and air production with her. Was this normal? Hell, no. Yet seeing her walk away opened up a yawning ache inside him and the feeling was so compelling that he had to take a minute. Shake his head and clear it. Remind himself that he'd see her again in a few short hours.

Well, they wouldn't be *short* hours, apparently, but a few hours.

In the meantime, he had something to do. Something important.

Too bad he couldn't remember what it was.

The feeling of Livia's lips moving beneath his? Now that, he could remember. Maybe he should take a quick dip into the icy river and clear the remnants of her touch out of his thrumming blood. Maybe then his mind would be able to access the other parts of his life, of which there were many.

Think, man. He'd already met with the production manager this morning and spent an hour walking the vines, checking the grapes...

Lunch! He was supposed to be having a late lunch with his mother and daughter up at the B and B, where his parents lived in a private wing away from the guests and spent a lot of their time.

Right.

By the time he got there and made his way to the small family dining room off the huge kitchen, however, Kendra was gone and Mom, who had a disquieting gleam in her eyes, was clearing the dishes.

"Sorry, Mom." He paused to kiss her cheek before taking his seat at the weathered oak table that sat in front of an enormous bay window overlooking the pool in the distance and, beyond that, the tennis courts. "What'd she eat today?"

Kendra, with the unerringly faulty taste buds of a six-year-old, ignored all the delicious farmer's market produce, fresh fish and gourmet dishes the chefs prepared for the guests here, preferring to eat chicken fingers, hot dogs, pizza and peanut butter and jelly sandwiches in an endless and disgusting rotation. They'd long ago given up trying to fight city hall and instead focused on sneaking her an occasional carrot stick or grape.

"PB&J." Mom made a face in case there was any doubt about her thoughts on this particular selection. "But I did get her to drink a big glass of milk and eat some pineapple slices."

"Fresh?" he asked hopefully.

"Canned."

Sighing, he accepted the soup and salad she passed across the table to him—creamy lobster bisque, field greens with grilled salmon and balsamic vinaigrette and all the hot sourdough rolls he could eat, which was usually about four—and bowed his head for grace. When he sensed her hovering over him, waiting to pounce, he kept his head down for a few seconds longer. Eventually that just became silly, and his bread was getting cold.

He braced himself for the coming inquisition, took a fortifying bite of soup and decided to take the bull by the horns. "Something on your mind?"

Mom looked around from where she'd begun wiping the counters down, all bewildered innocence in an Emmy-caliber performance. "Hmm—what? No. Why do you ask?"

Snorting, he tore into a roll and reached for the butter.

"Kendra went to find her dinosaur books—" He kept chewing as his mother spoke. They were getting closer now. "—because she wanted to show them to Livia

Blake—" almost there "—and she seems to be a lovely woman. I thought she'd be one of those Hollywood diva types, but she wasn't like that at all. She's very good with children, but she wasn't too happy with *you*. Said you were rude to her or something. What's that about? You're never rude to anyone, especially paying guests. What do you think of her?"

Bam. There it was. The pink elephant in the room.

Mom had sniffed something in the air and was now on the trail of a potential romance for her widowed son. Any roads that might lead to additional grandchildren must be followed with due diligence—that was the woman's philosophy in a nutshell.

Shrugging, he focused all his attention on pouring a glass of iced tea from the pitcher without spilling a drop. Fortunately, his hands didn't shake. Unfortunately, he couldn't prevent the hot wave of…something from crawling over his face and making him feel sheepish.

"She's fine."

"Fine?" Gaping, Mom tossed that sponge on the counter.

"Fine."

"That's all you have to say, Hunter Chambers? Or should I call you J.R.?"

"That's all I have to say, Mama Chambers."

Mom returned to wiping all nearby hard surfaces with a frustrated vengeance; she hated it when he stonewalled her. You'd think she'd stop with the pointed questions now that he was damn near forty, but no.

"Well, I like her. Kendra really likes her—"

"Willard likes her, too."

That was when that shrewd gaze zeroed in on him, cutting off all means of escape. "I'm guessing you like her best of all."

He shoveled salad into his mouth, willing her not to notice his burning cheeks. "Guess all you want. It's a free countr—"

Ah, shit.

She walked over, cupped his face in her soft hand like he was three years old again and gave him a shot of that maternal understanding that always made him want to press his face to her belly and lean in for a comforting hug that lasted two to three hours. He was lucky to have a mother like this and he knew it. He just wished she didn't know him so damn well.

"It's time, Buddy Boy," she said gently. "It's time."

That old familiar misery inside him woke up, yawned and stretched and reported for duty. Though it might take a break for an hour or two here or there, or even a few days when he was lucky, misery always checked back in with him and kept him from getting too far away.

In the three years since he, Annette and Kendra had climbed into that car for a day trip down to San Francisco and only he and Kendra climbed out alive, he'd learned to master misery a little bit, to keep it at arm's length by focusing on something else like, say, Kendra or the winery, and he tried to do that now. To shrug it away and laugh.

"You're not fooling anyone." He smiled around his

sip of iced tea but it felt strained and weak, as though his mouth muscles weren't strong or experienced enough to manage expressions of pleasure. "You just want more grandchildren."

"I just want you to be happy."

As if that wasn't a big enough test of his emotional control, she bent down and kissed him on the cheek, leaving a powdery fresh scent in her wake. And he damn near lost it.

Was he allowed to be happy when Annette was dead and his daughter had been motherless since the tender age of three? Really? Who said? Where was the fairness in that? Why did he get his mother's blessing on living his life when Annette was gone and he'd had to scatter her ashes down into the vine-strewn valley she'd loved so much? Wouldn't it be better if he kept his existence utilitarian and tormented into the indefinite future? And if his whole life didn't need to be given over to grief and penance, wasn't a mere three years way too short a time to mourn the wife he'd loved and lost to a slick road?

This time the casual shrug and smile didn't come so fast. They didn't come at all, especially after he stared up into the bottomless understanding in his mother's wise eyes.

"Is it that easy, Mom? Being happy?"

"It might be." She dimpled at him in that reassuring way she had, opening the door to the possibility that things may not be quite as bad as he feared. "With the right woman, it just might be." Disappearing into the pantry, she left him to digest this kernel of wisdom in peace.

Until his father banged into the kitchen through the back door, stomping his work boots on the mat to get rid of mud and smacking his leather gloves against his dirt-smudged jeans. Harvesttime and walking the vines always got his juices flowing, but that did not, Hunter knew, explain the brilliant sparks of excitement in the old man's eyes.

"What's up?" Hunter wondered.

Dad gave one of those low, appreciative whistles that never needed an explanation, especially among the male of the species. "I just got a glimpse of that model, Livia Baker—"

"Blake," Hunter said, starting to get the picture and trying not to laugh.

"—and let me tell you—"

Mom reappeared in the doorway of the pantry, carrying a jar of cookies and glaring.

Dad's cheeks flushed but to his credit, he never missed a beat. "—that she is nowhere near as pretty as she looks in the magazines, poor thing. They must do a whole lot of airbrushing with that one. Oh, hey, honey. Can I have a cookie?"

"Absolutely not," Mom said, stalking through the kitchen and into the main dining room, leaving the door to close behind her with an irritated flap.

"She's here! She's here! Miss Livia's here!"

Livia, who was used to creating a stir when she

entered a room and had stepped out of more limos, walked more red carpets and runways and stared into the flashing lights of more paparazzi cameras than she could possibly count or remember, paused at the corner of the Chambers family private terrace, Willard on her heels, feeling a) humbled by Kendra's exuberant greeting and b) nervous.

Really nervous.

She hesitated, taking in the sweeping valley view, the planters overflowing with greenery, the wrought-iron table with market umbrella, the flickering white candles, a pair of older adults and…oh, God, there he was, over in the bar area opening a bottle of wine and studying her with those unreadable eyes.

Hunter Chambers, the man who'd planted such a fine kiss on her that her lips were still tingling hours later. *Okay, girl. Pull it together and don't stare unless you want his family to think you're a complete and unmitigated flake.* Hoping for the best, she opened her mouth and prayed that her voice cooperated.

"Hi, sweetie!" Bending just in time to catch the girl as she hurled herself at Livia's legs, Livia took a moment to wonder if she'd worn the right outfit. "It's good to see you!"

Over in the four-star restaurant on the main terrace, the female diners were wearing a lot of black. Black dresses, black slacks, black pumps—black, black, black, black…and, yes, black. But she'd only brought the one LBD (little black dress), and it was too much for a small dinner that included a child wearing—she glanced down at Kendra for a closer look—a T-shirt with several colorful dinosaurs on it, including a T. rex, some terrible flying thing with teeth, a triceratops and a legend that read It's More Fun in the Cretaceous Period.

Yeah. If there were kids in T-shirts, she didn't need to be wearing Chanel. So she'd scrounged around in her suitcase and produced a crocheted blue sweater, which she'd thrown over the off-white sundress she'd be wearing for the rest of the trip. It would have to do.

And, oh, man, was she crazy, or was there something special about this little girl who was so sturdy and strong and smelled so sweetly of baby lotion and fruity shampoo? Planting a kiss atop the snarled curls of her little head, Livia pulled her closer and went ahead and wished it—that she had one at home just like this. Yes, she did. In fact, she'd give back a good portion of the millions she'd made last year if only she had a little balance in her life, a little more peaceful quiet and a lot more hugs just like this one.

Without warning, it was over. Having had enough affection even if Livia wasn't quite ready to let go yet, Kendra pulled free and yanked on Livia's hand, towing her to the table. "You can sit right there by me, okay? See the place card? I made it. So that's your seat."

Livia peered at the place card in question. Kendra had clearly used every crayon in the box producing this one, which had surprisingly good flowers on it and her tragically misspelled name in neat green letters: *Leviah.*

Livia stifled a delighted laugh.

"And I brought my dinosaur encyclopedia and some other books and you can see—" Mrs. Chambers stepped forward, put an indulgent hand on her granddaughter's shoulder and steered her a few steps away from Livia. She made a discreet face that Kendra wasn't able to see.

"You probably won't believe this, Livia, but I swear we only gave this child one pot of coffee today."

"I don't mind," Livia said, laughing and accepting Mrs. Chambers's kiss on the cheek. "I love to talk dinosaurs. And thank you for having me for dinner."

"Thank you for coming." Mrs. Chambers held her arm wide, drawing her husband into the conversation. He was tall and handsome, like his son, and wore rimless glasses along with a white dress shirt and dark pants that made him seem like a charming college professor. "Livia Blake, this is my husband, Hunter."

Mr. Chambers took one game step forward, held his hand out and then lapsed into what appeared to be dumbstruck paralysis. His unblinking and wide-eyed gaze latched on to Livia's face and wouldn't, Livia suspected, let go even if a flying saucer buzzed by overhead.

"I…" he said, and then apparently lost his train of thought.

Livia waited a beat to give him the chance to recover, but…nothing.

There was no helping it; she laughed. It'd been a while since she'd had quite this effect on someone and she'd be lying if she said it didn't make her feel good. Grabbing his hand, she shook it.

"So nice to meet you, Mr. Chambers. You have a beautiful winery."

"I…yes, I…thanks, and…nice to—"

"Oh, for God's sake," Mrs. Chambers hissed. "I asked you not to embarrass the family."

Mr. Chambers flushed, shot an abashed look at his wife and swallowed audibly. Livia had high hopes for a recovery and an actual sentence or two out of him, but when he looked her in the face again, he reassumed his deer-in-the-headlights expression.

"I—" he began again. "I—"

"Okay, Dad." Hunter made a quiet appearance beside them. Extracting his father's hand from Livia's, he passed the old man off to Mrs. Chambers, who yanked him over to the side for what looked like a pretty good talking-to. "That's enough staring at the beautiful woman for now. You can try again later if you stop drooling on your shirt."

Livia smiled after Mr. Chambers (what a sweetheart!), at least until Hunter slid his palm against hers and twined her fingers in his strong grip. As though they'd done it multiple times daily for the last twenty years, he took her hand to lead her to the table and it felt stunning and yet absolutely natural.

Heat trickled over her face, making it hard to look at him. When she risked a sidelong glance, she discovered a wry glint in his eyes, which were like polished copper in this light.

"You have a strange effect on the males in this family, I've noticed."

Oh, man. More flirting. Her foolish heart was going to give out before she even got to sample their wine. "Is that so?"

"You know it's so."

She paused, letting him pull out the designated chair for her before she sat. Some little devil made her glance over her shoulder and peep up at him from under her lashes.

"But you're not kicking me out...?"

"Oh, no." Leaning closer on the pretext of scootching her in, he let his nose skim her hair in a brushing touch that made her toes curl in her strappy sandals. "You smell way too good to kick out. Have some wine."

He passed her a glass of something rich and red, showing no sign that he had any idea of his disturbing power over her or how he made her skin tingle with absolutely no effort on his part. She, meanwhile, wondered when this intriguing man was going to kiss her again and what she could do to speed up the process.

That was when Livia knew she was in trouble.

Deep, serious and unavoidable trouble.

Chapter 6

The edible part of dinner was wonderful, a feast of everything that was fresh, colorful and delicious: olives from the groves surrounding the grapes, salad, caviar on sourdough crostini, grilled salmon with parmesan risotto, cheeses and fruits and a chocolate torte for dessert. To Livia's immense pleasure, she even got Kendra, who was apparently a finicky eater, to try the risotto.

"I don't like it," Kendra said, glaring at the single bite Livia had scooped onto the fork for her.

"You didn't even try it. I don't see how you can eat a hot dog and not try any of this fantastic food your grandmother cooked, Kendra," Livia told her. "Taste one bite. It's sort of like macaroni and cheese."

"Well…okay."

Around the table, there was a ripple of excitement as the girl took the bite and chewed, as though they'd all just witnessed the birth of a rare giant panda or something equally auspicious.

They waited. Kendra smiled. "Can I have some more, please?"

Everyone laughed with relief. In that delicious moment, Livia's gaze was drawn to Hunter's, and when he winked and mouthed *Thank you,* a shivering thrill filled her heart to bursting and she had to look away on the pretext of reaching for her goblet.

And the wine...

Livia drank two glasses of zinfandel produced by vines that were, they told her, over a hundred years old, and then enjoyed a chardonnay that Hunter claimed was so creamy because it tasted of butterscotch, with scents of pear and apple.

Ambrosia. Nectar of the gods. Liquid heaven.

Thinking about her agent's horrified reaction if she could see her eating and drinking like a starved sow at the trough, Livia shuddered. And had another slice of torte with an extra splash of raspberry sauce.

Wonderful as the food was, though, it was the company that made the dinner. As the sun settled on the horizon and Hunter watched her from across the table, the candlelight flickering against his eyes, she learned all about cooking from Mrs. Chambers and winemaking from Mr. Chambers, once he recovered his tongue and the powers of speech, and dinosaurs from Kendra.

After two hours of the food, wine and laughter, Livia

could claim, with absolute certainty, that she wasn't anxious to leave this enchanted valley and go back to L.A. anytime soon.

Displaying what she was beginning to think of as a delightful possessive streak, Hunter took her hand again—right in front of his parents, he took her hand!—and spoke to his daughter, who was naming the dinosaurs on her T-shirt for the second or third time that night.

"Say good-night to Miss Livia, Kendra. I'm taking her for a walk and it's time for you to go to bed. We already talked about you sleeping in your bed here tonight."

Kendra frowned, her pointed index finger hovering around the parasaurolophus covering her navel. "But I don't want to go to bed."

Hunter folded his arms across his chest, clearly girding his loins for battle but determined to be patient. "I understand that. It's still bedtime."

"But—" Kendra began.

"Maybe," Livia interjected, slipping between girl and father, who were now wearing identical intransigent looks, "we could play in the dragon's den tomorrow after school—"

Kendra began to hop from one foot to the other, glowing with supreme happiness.

"*If* you go to bed without giving your father a hard time," Livia finished.

Kendra's expression soured, and her hovering foot hit the flagstone with an annoyed stomp. "But I—"

"Take it or leave it." A sudden spark of maternal instinct made Livia put her hands on her hips, the way her mother always did when she wanted to scare Livia and her brothers spitless, and it seemed to work. "Last chance."

"Okay," Kendra said in a hurry, as though she feared Livia would rescind the offer forever. "Okay, okay." She turned to Mrs. Chambers. "Can you read me a story first, Grandma? Pleaaaaase?"

"And the stalling begins," Hunter murmured in Livia's ear. She stifled a grin.

"I certainly will," Mrs. Chambers said. "Livia, you come back real soon now, you hear?"

Livia kissed her cheek. "If you feed me like that again, I'll be here for three or four meals a day."

"That'd be fine with us," Mr. Chambers said eagerly, earning himself a big eye roll from his wife.

The goodbyes continued, stretching into a procedure that was beginning to remind Livia of the "Goodnight, John-Boy" portion of *The Waltons*. The family, especially Kendra, didn't seem to want to let her go. She didn't want to go. Except that she was excruciatingly aware of Hunter's thumb stroking over the back of her hand and of the frustrated tension thrumming through his big body. Feeling the same delicious agitation herself, she recognized it for what it was: he wanted to be alone with her. Now.

Finally he lost all patience. "You will see the poor woman tomorrow, people. She's not going to disappear overnight, okay?" He didn't bother keeping the exasperation out of his voice. "Can you let me walk her to her cottage, please? Kendra, you have school tomorrow, so you need to get cracking."

After a last whiny response from Kendra, he gave Livia's hand a gentle tug and they were off, skirting the terrace wall and heading through the cooling night and into the relative darkness of the path that led to her guesthouse.

Livia was still grinning with a ridiculous amount of delight. This dinner had felt just like the ones back home in small-town Georgia, with relatives crammed around a table groaning with good food, all of them talking at once. None of the fancy-schmancy dinners at trendy L.A. restaurants she'd been to lately could top that. Please. Most of the time, those places only served half a spear of asparagus with some unidentifiable sauce in a starburst pattern on the plate and called it a meal.

Yeah. She wasn't anxious to go back home.

"Your family is so great," she gushed. "I wasn't sure your father was ever going to talk to me, but when he finally—"

Midstride, and without warning, Hunter swung her around, into his arms and up against the hard length of his body. The shock rippled through her and she only had time for a quick *"Oh, God,"* before his mouth found hers and they were kissing—urgently, sweetly, amazingly—in the shadowed privacy of a huge tree at the edge of the grounds, where terrace and stone path gave way to hill.

Livia crooned and fell deeper into sensation, her

body's reactions so far outside her control they may as well have been operating from different time zones. He smelled like sunshine and air, earthy outdoors and fresh, clean man, and the delicious tartness of red wine in his mouth made her want to swallow him whole, right now.

Other men had tried this kind of thing with her before, most notably the arrogant rapper-turned-fashion-designer who thought that a couple of text messages, a nice dinner and a hundred-dollar bouquet of lilies entitled him to a blow job in the limo on the way home. For them, she had a verbal smack-down. For Hunter, she had a willing body and a mouth that opened eagerly to let his tongue slip inside.

God, he felt good. She wanted…

He pulled back but his hands kept their hold on her face, and his fingers relentlessly massaged her nape, driving her abso-freaking-lutely wild.

"I needed that."

"So did I," she breathed.

"Should I apologize?"

Huh? "For what? Being the world's greatest kisser?"

Another little licking kiss was her reward for that compliment, and she mewled and surged up, closer, wanting more. He pulled back for a second time and studied her with a troubled gleam in his eyes.

"Is there some billionaire planning to pick you up on his private jet for a luxurious trip to Fiji I should know about?"

Was he jealous? How fun!

"Wow. That's the longest sentence I've ever heard you string together."

"Is there?"

"No."

"Are you just killing time until one shows up?"

What? *"No,"* she said, starting to get annoyed.

His eyes narrowed. "Maybe you're just killing time between parties," he mused. "Taking a little break here in the country and gearing up for the next premiere or something?"

Okay, hold up. What was with him and the never-ending accusations of bad behavior? Were these garden-variety insecurities because she was rich and famous and he wasn't? Or had he heard those tired rumors about her party-girl reputation?

"For your information," she snapped, "I severely curtailed my partying several years ago, when one of my friends was injured by a drunk driver. I rarely drink. Tonight was an exception. Is there anything else you'd like to accuse me of since your opinion of me is so low? You think I'm, what—a diva, an airhead, a party girl, oh, and a dog- and child-hurter. Anything else?"

Gazes locked, they engaged in a wary stare-down for several tense beats and then some of the sudden harshness bled out of his expression. A wry smile curled one edge of his lips and, taking her hand again, he kissed it.

"Like I mentioned," he said by way of apology, "you do strange things to me."

Lord, she knew that feeling, didn't she? "I don't believe that's *quite* what you said."

"That's all the confession you're getting out of me. Other than it's hard for me to believe I'd get this lucky."

Huh?

Mr. Presumptuous needed to be smacked back to earth, didn't he? Arching a brow, she folded her arms across her chest. "Pardon me, but who says you're going to get lucky? That remains to be seen, doesn't it?"

She put a lot of frost in her voice, which was pretty funny since she'd been a kiss and a rub away from orgasm mere seconds ago, and he'd accomplished that fully clothed and without a bed.

"Does it?"

Man, he was nothing but trouble, saying it without male arrogance and making it sound like genuine puzzlement. *Gee, Livia, are you really so delusional that you honestly think we can keep a lid on the explosive passion we're feeling right here? Wow, you should get that checked out by a professional.*

"Yes," she lied.

"A thousand apologies. Let me rephrase. I can't believe I'd get lucky enough for an amazing woman like you to wander across my path, and I didn't even have to leave home."

Oh, man.

She wished he wouldn't make her foolish heart skitter like that.

His cheeks dimpled with a repressed smile. "Better?"

Hitching up her chin, she tried to look haughty and no doubt failed spectacularly. "Maybe."

He grinned and took her hand to get them started moving again. She fell into step, matching his long stride with no trouble, but sudden doubts and fears followed right behind her, bringing a chilling dose of reality with them.

"What are we doing, Hunter?"

Staring up at his profile as he studied the path ahead, she saw the subtle tightening of his jaw and knew he understood the question. Still, he chose not to answer it.

"We're taking a walk."

"I'm only here for a few days," she reminded him.

"I know that."

"I don't do casual relationships," she continued. "I'm past that young and stupid phase of my life, and I never handled them well, anyway."

"Got it."

Was he always this frustratingly evasive? "So what are we doing with each other?"

He twitched his shoulders, shrugging this away the way he might get rid of an aggressive fly at a picnic. "I don't know. My crystal ball's in the shop."

Okay. Enough with the walking. Yanking her hand free, she darted in front of him, giving him the choice of stopping or plowing over her. He stopped. Grudgingly.

And huffed out an exasperated sigh that did nothing to soothe her increasing agitation.

"I don't think you understand that I can't just—"

"You talk a lot," he told her. "And you think too much."

He thought *this* was talking a lot? Boy, was he in for a rude awakening.

"Get used to it," she warned.

"Anything else I should get used to?"

"Yes. I'm a big control freak. Very anal-retentive. I make lists. I check things twice. I don't just make willy-nilly decisions without thinking about the consequences."

"That's the city in you. Here in the country, we know we can't control the weather and we can't control every opportunity that pops up along the way."

Something about the O-word made ice form in her gut. "Is that what I am? An opportunity? So now you can cross 'had wild sex with a supermodel' off your bucket list and move on to the next item?"

He stilled, his displeasure so obvious and overwhelming it was like a fire hose blast to the face. She had to fight the urge to duck and run.

"Is that what you think about me?"

It was hard to hold his gaze and not shrink inside her skin like a chastised teenager. That low, irritated voice of his must be *very* effective in keeping Kendra in line, poor child, because it made Livia feel like a slime-trailing slug, and she was a grown woman.

"No," she said, staring at the ground.

Considering her for a minute, mollified for now, he tilted his head and tapped his index finger against his lips. "You want a formal declaration, Livia? Is that what this is about?"

"A formal decl—"

"How about this?" He swallowed roughly, making his Adam's apple dip, and she seriously wished it wasn't so dark outside because she'd swear he was blushing. "For the first time since my wife died, I'm interested enough in a woman to let her spend a little time with my daughter and introduce her to my parents."

"Oh," she said, her heart skittering to a stop.

"I've never gotten involved with a guest at the winery, and if I did want to get involved with a woman, it wouldn't normally be with a celebrity who lives four hundred miles away and is wanted by most of the men in the English-speaking world, most of whom have way more money than I do."

Livia's stare froze into a gape.

"However, I am so intrigued by you that my doubts seem ridiculous. And, in case you didn't notice, the train has already left the station on something developing between us. So, if all that makes sense to you, and if you're on board with me not being able to predict the future, I'd really like to get to know you better while you're here. Okay?"

She nodded frantically.

"Can we walk now?" he asked.

"Yes."

"Thank God for that." He started off again.

Undone, Livia gripped his hand tighter and leaned her head against his shoulder, knowing that if she wasn't careful—if she wasn't really, *really* careful—she was going to fall crazy in love with this man.

Chapter 7

"I want you to see something," Hunter said as they turned a bend in the path.

"Oh, yeah?" Livia lifted her head and stared up at him with avid interest, as though he might whip out a Ferrari and present it to her. That was one of the things he really liked about her, the enthusiasm that made everything feel like a great adventure. Was she always like this? So bright-eyed and enthralling? "Is someone finally going to give me an official tour of the winery?"

"We can do that tomorrow."

"What is it, then?—ooohhhh. *Stars*."

They'd come to the hillside's edge, where the path ended, opening up to a sweeping view of the dark valley and, beyond that, the gentle beginnings of the mountains. Above all that, a sprinkling of stars glittered like diamonds spilled on black velvet.

"Oh, my God." She tipped her head toward the sky, gaping with open delight. "How amazing."

Grinning, he wrapped his arms around her from behind, rested his cheek against her temple and enjoyed the feel and smell of her. How did she maintain that country girl's spirit of delight in simple things even though her modeling career had no doubt molded her into the most sophisticated woman who'd ever crossed his path? Why did this woman thrill him beyond all reason?

"Is this okay?"

He nuzzled the sweet column of her long neck and prayed she didn't push him away anytime soon because there was a serious question in his mind about whether he could let her go or not. But, in answer, she relaxed against him and rested her arms atop his to keep him close.

"It is not okay at all. I plan to call the police and have you arrested for assault in a couple hours or so."

"Well." He shifted enough for his raging erection to settle into the cleft of her amazing ass, just so she could see what she did to him. For emphasis, he ran his tongue up the side of her neck and nipped her earlobe. "As long as I'm already in trouble…"

Her breath did an excited little hitching thing that went a long way toward unraveling what normally passed as his self-control. That was strange and problematic. Self-control and he were buddies. They hung out with discipline and perseverance. As a gang, the four of them managed both his winery and his daughter, and kept his dog from being any more unruly than he already was.

That made for smooth sailing, right? *Keep your nose to the grindstone, Hunter, build your winery and raise your daughter. Keep the blinders on and look neither left nor right. Other people might have more of a life, yeah, but not you. Fun with a woman is strictly off-limits to you, so don't even think about it.*

Normally, that was all well and good, and he embraced his duties with enthusiasm.

But normally he didn't have Livia in his arms, and damn…she felt good. Really good. So good that he wasn't in any hurry to return to the house and tuck his daughter in bed. Nor was he anxious to attack the paperwork waiting for him after that. Nor, come to think of it, did he see any need to work like an indentured servant tomorrow. Ownership had its perks, and he was pretty sure that the winery wouldn't turn to salt and dust if he took tomorrow off.

He wanted to play, just this once, and he wanted to play with Livia.

In more ways than one.

The fact that this woman could make him think unprecedented thoughts like these should have made him run for the hills. Instead, it made him feel…he felt…it was like…

He felt alive.

With Livia, he felt as though he'd put one foot through the door back into the land of the living. Was that allowed when his wife was dead? Probably not, but until a bouncer showed up to throw him out, he'd spend as much time with her as possible.

Livia swiveled her hips, grinding into him, and this time it was his breath that did the hitching, especially when a female murmur of appreciation hummed in her throat.

"Wow." Underneath her sudden breathlessness, he heard the strain in her voice as she tried to keep this light and easy when really this growing thing between them was enough to scare any thinking person to death. "Do the stars always get you this excited?"

Nuzzling his way to her ear, he whispered the truth.

"This is all about you, Livia, and you know it."

If a person could melt and stiffen at the same time, that's what she did. It was like she wanted to relax and enjoy this moment with him, but wouldn't give herself permission.

He could almost hear her doubts cranking like a hamster on a wheel. "There you go thinking again. Maybe you should ease up on that a little."

"What, relax? Me?"

"Aren't you on vacation?"

She grinned, causing her cheeks to plump against his lips. This was nothing less than an invitation to kiss her sweet skin again, so he did. "It's hard to relax when I'm always dashing off to do the next thing. Plus, it's hard to relax in a great new place when I'm anxious to explore it."

"Anything else?"

"Yeah." She paused, apparently fighting the urge to hold tight to her secrets. "It's hard to relax when you're touching me."

Was that it? No. His gut told him there was more, and he wanted all of it.

"Because..." he prompted.

Turning her head just enough, she looked him in the eye and let herself be vulnerable. "Because you make my skin hum."

Something happened between them in that moment. Maybe it was the connection of their gazes or her willingness to let him get a little closer or, hell, the starlight. He couldn't pin it down to one single cause. All he knew was that a tenderness for her opened up inside him, blossoming like a daylily in the sun, and the feeling was familiar and not unwelcome. He'd felt it before, with Kendra, of course, and he'd felt it with...

Whoa.

Time to slow this down a little.

But...one more kiss first. He had to.

So, letting all of her go except her hand—he wasn't made of stone, and he could only control his skin's craving for her so much—he smiled a little to tell her it was all right and brushed her lips with his.

Then he towed her to the nearest wrought-iron bench, where they sat. And then, because you couldn't properly stargaze while sitting upright, he eased her back until her head was on his lap and he could stroke the fine hair at her temple while they talked.

* * *

Bit by bit, Hunter felt the tension ease out of her and he considered it a triumph, something as big and significant as the invention of movable type or the discovery of penicillin.

"Do you have stars like this in L.A.?" he asked after a while, because some foolish and insecure corner of his brain needed to know that he and Napa had things to offer her that the City of Angels—and the rest of the world, for that matter—didn't.

"Who knows?" she answered. "No one in L.A. has been able to see the sky in living memory."

"The smog isn't that bad, is it?"

"Not really. But this is spectacular." She pointed at something that held her rapt attention. "And there's the North Star—"

"Actually, that's Jupiter."

"Jupiter," she murmured, her body loosening a little more. "I've never seen it before."

It made him happy to introduce her to something new. Ridiculously happy. Too happy, because the feeling could easily become addictive and he was already addicted to both her smile and the feeling of his hands on her body and hers on his.

For a while there was a wonderful silence broken only by the occasional rustle of the wind through the trees. She stared at the stars in the sky, he stared at their reflection in her gorgeous dark eyes, and life was good. Quiet didn't bother him. He'd never been one to talk just for the sake of hearing his own voice. But then it occurred to him that he had everything to learn about her and only a few days to do it, so he'd better get started.

"Tell me one thing about you," he said.

Her brow scrunched. "One thing?"

"One thing I need to know to really get you. Other than you love baseball."

She grinned, her confusion clearing. "I'm from small-town Georgia."

Being from northern California himself, this needed some clarification.

"And therefore…?"

"And therefore I'm a country girl at heart. I like peaches fresh off the tree and my mama's snap beans drenched in butter. Also, lumpy grits drenched in butter and biscuits drenched in butter. If you don't have biscuits, I'll take cornbread, but I prefer the biscuits. Or I'll just take the butter. I like to have my sisters and brothers around, with all their screaming children, and it's best to sleep with the windows open so you can get the cool night air. It's good for sleeping." She paused and seemed to think it over. "That's about it."

"That's you in a nutshell?"

"That's me in a nutshell."

This information needed a little bit of analysis; the scientist in him required it. "You didn't mention anything about your career."

"Hmm. Guess I didn't, did I?"

Wow. For someone who made money hand over fist, that was really strange. And so was the fact that everything she'd just said was inconsistent with modeling as he understood it.

"Correct me if I'm wrong, but is anything you just named possible as, one, a model, and, two, a model based on the West Coast? I mean, do you get down South much? And do they serve grits to the models in Paris during Fashion Week?"

Her snort and dramatic eye roll needed no interpretation. "Honey, if anyone in the business knew I ate grits, they'd probably cancel all my contracts tomorrow. Grits go right to the hips."

Well, he liked her hips just fine, thanks, but he didn't want the conversation to get diverted because this seemed important. "Answer the questions, please."

Something in her expression dimmed. She shrugged, studiously avoiding his gaze. "It's my life," she said simply. "My career has plusses and minuses. Everyone's does."

He kept quiet. Naturally, she noticed.

"Oh, come on." Turning her head, she frowned up at him. "Are you telling me there's nothing about your job you don't like?"

"I could do without the mud."

"That's it?" she demanded.

How could he explain how he loved it here? It wasn't something to quantify in ten words or less, or even a few paragraphs, but the grapes were in his blood. Corny, but true. He needed the hills and the river, the vines and the olives and the air.

Some people lived in concrete jungles with canned

air, traffic and smog, but not him, not ever. The idea of being far away from the leaves and the harvest was enough to make him break into a sweat. If he didn't have to worry about parasites, pests and the weather, he'd think he'd died and gone to heaven.

"That's it." He smiled wryly, telling it like it was without the varnish. "I'm a farmer. I love my farm. That's what you need to know about me."

Snuggling closer, she settled her head in the crook of his arm, rested her cheek against his belly and circled her arms around his waist. Her lids fluttered with drowsiness, reminding him of Kendra at bedtime, fighting sleep.

"I love your farm, too," she murmured, trying to pout. "I only hope someone'll take me on a tour of it before I leave."

He stroked her hair again, fighting the growing tenderness he felt for her and losing big. "I'll show it to you first thing in the morning, baby. If you keep working on relaxing. Deal?"

"Deal."

She was true to her word. After a couple minutes, her breathing evened out, and before he knew it, she was asleep. Content in a way he hadn't been for years, he sat there with her long past the time he should have returned to his house and to work.

The pounding continued.

Livia crawled out from under the delightful jumble of warm linens and cracked one bleary eye open against the faint predawn light trying to creep past the fluttering curtains. The open window, which had seemed like such a brilliant idea when she went to bed, now let in an arctic chill that would soon create conditions ripe for icicles and frostbite. It also didn't help that she'd cleverly worn only a tank top and panties last night, thinking that'd be more comfortable than the new nightgown she'd brought. The floor was a frozen lake for her poor tootsies—her flip-flops were nowhere to be seen—and she hadn't bothered packing a robe.

Some idiot, meanwhile, was trying to break down her door.

Cursing, she hurried through the cottage, ran into an end table that'd moved two feet to the left sometime during the night and peeked out the nearest window to see what the big freaking emergency was and who she needed to blame and possibly kill for this rude awakening.

Oh, God. Hunter. It was *Hunter. Nooooo.*

He looked annoyingly bright-eyed beneath his baseball cap (today it was the Pittsburgh Crawfords), and was dressed in jeans and a jacket. His hands were filled with two disposable cups of coffee, which made her wonder what the heck he'd been knocking with.

Gasping, she let the curtain drop, ducked back into the shadows and wished she could hide beneath the nearest rug. Maybe if she was really still and quiet, he'd go away and—

"I saw you," he called from the other side of the door.

Of *course* he saw her.

With no other choice available, she sucked it up and tried to be a woman about this. All she could do was sweep her hands through the rat's nest snarl of her hair and thank the stars she had good skin, although what woman on earth couldn't benefit from a quick swipe of lip gloss? Ah, well. No time for that now.

Swearing she'd get even with him for this if it was the last thing she ever did, she cracked the door open enough to stick her head out and glare.

He grinned, the bastard. "Good morning."

"It's the crack of dawn. Less than the crack of dawn. The roosters haven't even had their coffee yet."

"I thought you wanted your tour today."

"I do want my tour. You said 'first thing,' which to me means sometime after the sun actually rises. I'm on vacation."

The bright amusement in his expression left no room for sympathy for her lack of sleep. Of course, he didn't know that after he'd woken her from that wonderful spot with her head resting on his lap, walked her back here and left her with a chaste kiss on the doorstep, she'd spent several hours writhing around the bed in sexual frustration.

She'd wondered, in no particular order, whether he was sleeping, what, if anything, he was sleeping in, what kind of bed he had, whether he was thinking of her and whether he wanted them both to be in the same bed anywhere near as much as she did. The result was a solid fifteen minutes of sleep for her, which was something less than what she was used to, even with her frantic work schedule.

"We start early here," he informed her.

"Have mercy," she begged.

His smile dimmed, leaving behind that naked intensity that made her skin sizzle. "I can't." The sudden roughening of his voice signaled that maybe he was struggling, too, that maybe he'd also been doing some serious yearning. "I had a tough time sleeping. I wanted today to start so I could get back to you."

Breathing suddenly got a whole lot more difficult. "Oh," she said in a stunning display of eloquence.

"Did you sleep?"

God. It was so hard to think when he looked at her like that, as though her face held the answers to all his prayers and he could study her forever. She shook her head, hating to be so honest but unable to deny him anything.

A deepening of his dimples told her that she'd just made him happy, and that made her happy. Like a hormonal junior high schooler who'd been caught passing a note to her crush, she flushed to the roots of her hair.

"Here's your coffee. Get dressed, okay?"

Turning to go, he passed the cup to her and their fingers brushed. With that simple touch, all bets were off. He paused, his shoulders squaring off with a new tension that radiated out from him and tightened something deep inside her belly.

Then he turned back. "Just out of curiosity…what're you wearing?"

A nervous titter flew out of her mouth before she could choke it back.

"You're kidding."

The early morning shadows hit his face just right, heightening the gleam in his eye and making him wicked. Dangerous. Irresistible.

"Do I look like I'm kidding?"

Absolutely not. "Panties," she said, swallowing hard. "A tank top."

His gaze, speculative now, flickered over her face and down the door, as though he wished his X-ray vision would kick in and help him see past her hiding place.

"That's it?"

"That's it."

A beat passed.

"Show me," he said softly.

Wow. She'd known that was coming, hadn't she? "I haven't been retouched and airbrushed," she warned.

He almost smiled. "I'll try not to scream."

She hesitated. In that moment, she had lots of options available to her. She could laugh and make another joke. She could slam the door in outrage. She could read him the riot act for suggesting such a thing.

She didn't do any of that.

Instead, she held his gaze, tossed her hair over her shoulder to shake off her wild nerves and stepped out from behind the door in all her nearly naked glory. He didn't look right away; he seemed far more interested in interpreting whatever he saw on her face. And then, at last, he looked down, his gaze gliding over her thin white tank and string bikinis with the ease of an Olympic skater on the ice.

Livia was comfortable with her body. As a model, she'd sashayed down runways all over the world, often more naked than clothed, and she'd posed for more than her share of magazine bikini shots. There'd even been that Times Square billboard of her in a teeny-tiny dress that'd barely covered her privates, selling her line of perfume.

None of that bothered her.

Hunter's eyes on her—now that bothered her. Correction: Hunter's gaze on her made her hot and bothered. It also made her ache with repressed needs until she felt the wet clench between her legs and the insistent swelling of her nipples.

He wasn't unaffected. All of his desire for her was obvious in his high color, glittering eyes and growing bulge in the front of his jeans. Watching him stare at her and feeling their effect on each other without even touching, she wondered how long they could hold out and why they even wanted to.

Some things couldn't be fought.

"Turn around," he said.

Putting one hand on her hip, she turned the way she'd been trained to do. There was an audible hitch in his breath and, spurred on by a tiny devil whispering in her ear, she looked over her shoulder at him. After a lingering look at her ass—judging by the open appreciation in his expression, he didn't think she had too much junk in her trunk, or anything like it—he stared into her face again.

That sharp electrical current flowed between them, making her feel like she'd been zapped by those defibrillator paddles they were always using on medical TV shows.

"Soon." His voice was raw now, husky with a passion that yanked against its restraints. "Okay?"

Soon? Was that, like—what? *Now?*

Now would be good, but she didn't want to be needy or brazen. Although that horse had, clearly, raced out of the barn hours ago.

Still, if he could be patient, then so could she. Sort of.

"Yeah," she said. "Soon."

He blinked and then dimpled again, breaking up some of the tension. Her mouth, on the other hand, had used up all of its skills on those last two words, so speaking was out of the question for her, at least for now.

Stepping back, he put some much needed distance between them. Not that it helped or anything, but it was a move in the right direction.

"Get going. Oh, and Livia?"

She waited.

"Don't forget to brush your teeth so I can kiss you good morning."

That snapped her out of it. Roaring with outrage, she slammed the door in his laughing face.

Chapter 8

"Help me lift it, please," Livia said.

Hunter stared at her with what was beginning to be a familiar mixture of exasperation and admiration. After a quick breakfast, they'd started their day in the pinot noir vines with the workers. He'd meant to show her how the picking was done and move on to the next stop on his nickel tour, but was that good enough for Livia, she of the bright eyes and endless curiosity? No. "I want to pick some," she'd said. So he'd found her a tub, showed her how to cradle the bunches and angle the curved blade just right and watched as she'd worked quickly and efficiently to fill it with purple grapes.

Now she wanted to lift the damn thing onto her head to carry it to the nearest gondola the way everyone else was doing.

"Livie." He chose his words with care because making it sound like it was too heavy for her would have the effect of doing the red cape shimmy in front of a charging bull. "These tubs weigh forty pounds."

As he could have predicted, this didn't slow her down any. Squatting to get a grip on the tub's handles, she gave him a purse-lipped glare.

"And therefore…?"

"And therefore I don't want you to get hurt. Your beautiful swan neck could snap in two and all your sponsors would come after me when you wind up stuck in traction for six months. I don't want to get sued."

Rolling her eyes, she stood, hefting the tub waist-high. "You're full of it, Chambers. Are you going to help me or not?"

Ernesto Sanchez, his foreman, chose that moment to stride by. Overflowing with amusement, he gave Hunter a "don't fight city hall" sort of shrug. "Do yourself a favor, *el mero mero*. Help *la muñeca*. She's picked more grapes than half the no-accounts on the payroll, you know? I think we should hire her."

Livia grinned. "*'La muñeca,'* eh? *Eres un coqueto.*" *You're a flirt.*

"*Siempre.*" *Always.* Winking at her, Ernesto disappeared down the path.

Feeling unaccountably annoyed, Hunter gave her a look. Was there no end to this woman's charms or talents? "You speak Spanish, eh?"

"Who doesn't?"

"Yeah, well." Lifting the stupid tub onto her head,

he made sure she had a good grip on it before he let go. "If you need someone to flirt with, *doll,* you can flirt with me."

Laughing and happy now—hell, if she liked manual labor so much, he should put her to work mopping the floors in the cave; that'd make her weep with joy—she called over her shoulder to him. "Yeah, but his accent is so sexy, big boss. Or do you prefer *el mero mero?*"

He got his own tub settled on his shoulder and grumbled. "I'd prefer getting out of this hot sun and not working so hard. A big boss shouldn't have to sweat."

Pausing, she swung around to face him, all sun-kissed enthusiasm and light. A waking dream that made his breath hitch and his thoughts scatter. "Have I mentioned how full of it you are? You love every second of being out in your fields."

Yeah, he did, but how did she know that? Was she that intuitive or did she have a secret window into his soul that no one else could access?

"I'm not that easy to read."

"Of course you are. I don't blame you, though." She glanced around, absorbing the natural beauty in every direction. "I'd never leave here if I were you."

"I never plan to."

She paused, a shadow flickering across her face that had nothing to do with the vines or the clouds. A thousand things went unspoken between them in that second, things he didn't want to think about until he absolutely had to. That he belonged here and she didn't. That while he would never live anywhere else, she did.

That this interlude between them, this moment, this connection, had a shelf life that would soon expire. That she would leave to return to her real life before he knew it, and he was beginning to fear she'd take the sun with her when she went.

But then she smiled again, delaying anything sad or serious between them.

"Let's go. I want to make sure I fill out the paperwork so I can get the employee health plan you owe me."

"So." Livia turned in a slow circle, feeling as though she'd been trapped in a Schwarzenegger/Stallone movie in which a thirty-foot wall of water would soon flood through, leaving little to no chance of survival. "Is this where the tortures are carried out?"

They stood inside one of the caves, which was a cool subterranean tunnel with naked overhead bulbs providing the only dim lighting. Shadows surrounded them on all sides, and she didn't peer at them too closely lest she spy an eight-legged critter and humiliate herself by screaming her fool head off.

Enormous wooden bins two rows deep lined either side of the path through the cave, and inside of each were about a hundred upside-down bottles of sleeping wine. The overall effect was more than a little eerie, and she was glad, in the farthest girly-girl corners of her heart, to have a big strong man with her if she had to spend time in this dungeon.

"This is where the wine rests until it's ready," Hunter told her.

"Have you ever been trapped in here?"

"No."

"Have the lights ever gone out on you?"

"Only that time Ethan flipped the switch on me."

"I can see him doing that."

He leaned against one of the bins, rested one ankle over the other and studied her with shrewd interest. "I forgot you know my brother from the show."

"That's right. *Paging the Doctor*. I was a proud guest star for a few episodes."

"Did you like acting?"

"It was fun, yeah. But I can tell by that scowl on your face that you're not wild about acting."

Caught, he crossed his arms over his chest and tried to shrug off his disapproval. "Ethan left the vineyard to become an actor. If that's what he wants to do with his life…" Another shrug.

"Oh, you're funny. If that's what he wants to do with his life, then—what? You support him a whopping two percent?"

The corners of his eyes crinkled but he withheld the full smile. She had the strong feeling he wished she couldn't read him so well or would at least stop doing it when he wasn't prepared.

"I'm not cut out for acting, or life in Hollywood," he told her. "But if that's what Ethan wants to do, then that's fine with me."

"He and Rachel seem very happy together, you know."

"Yeah. I can hear it in his voice when he calls."

"He's a good guy."

Hunter frowned. "You seem a little too fond of him. He didn't hit on you, did he?"

"Of *course* not," she said. "He was all over Rachel. I don't think he ever even looked at me."

He snorted as though this was as unlikely as surfing on Mars. "Get real."

She flushed and their gazes locked, leading into another of the deliciously silent moments they'd been sharing all morning. He had a way of studying her face that was so darkly, frankly appreciative that she suspected he'd swallow her whole if given half the chance.

The funny thing was, she couldn't wait to give him the chance.

They'd settled against opposite bins, both leaning, neither moving. The three or four feet of path separating them felt suddenly like a yawning canyon—way too wide and nearly impossible to cross.

"You know," she said, wishing he would take all decision making out of her hands and touch her. Hold her. Because she needed him to, even if she had a terrible time figuring out how to ask. "I brushed my teeth this morning. I even gargled. You never did give me my kiss." Trying to pout, she waited for him to react and meet her halfway. "Do I smell bad?"

"Your smell is not the issue, trust me. I love honey-suckle."

Whoa. Had he just correctly identified her body cream? "How did you—?"

"Like I told you. I'm a farmer. I know my flowers."

There was so much intensity in him; so much in the two of them together. If only she could figure out whether she should be running toward it or away from it. Right now she knew they were circling an issue that could be awkward, but did that really matter next to her consuming need to be close to him? Hell, even her pride was beginning to matter less.

"Are you dodging the question?" she wondered.

He cleared his throat and studied his shoes. Ran his hand over the top of his head and scrubbed his jaw. Showed every sign of being a man about to come out of his skin with agitation. The one thing he didn't do was come closer.

"The thing is," he said finally, his voice low and hoarse, "the more I kiss you, the harder it is for me to stop."

"Then don't stop."

There it was. Carte blanche. It didn't get much clearer than that, although of course they'd already discussed this a little bit this morning. He could have her any way he wanted her, as soon as he decided it was time. The rational part of her knew this was probably a bad idea that would lead to doom in the end. The rest of her just didn't care.

"We need to get this on the table right now." He stared at her, giving her a clear shot of the unhappiness in his eyes, the turmoil. "I'm not going to want you to go when your vacation is over."

KIMANI
ROMANCE

An Important Message from the Publisher

Dear Reader,

Because you've chosen to read one of our fine novels, I'd like to say "thank you"! And, as a special way to say thank you, I'm offering to send you two more Kimani™ Romance novels and two surprise gifts—absolutely FREE! These books will keep it real with true-to-life African American characters that turn up the heat and sizzle with passion.

Please enjoy the free books and gifts with our compliments...

Glenda Howard
For Kimani Press

Peel off Seal and Place Inside...

EDITOR'S
FREE GIFTS
SEAL
THANK YOU

We'd like to send you two free books to introduce you to Kimani™ Romance books. These novels feature strong, sexy women, and African-American heroes that are charming, loving and true. Our authors fill each page with exceptional dialogue, exciting plot twists, and enough sizzling romance to keep you riveted until the very end!

KIMANI ROMANCE...LOVE'S ULTIMATE DESTINATION

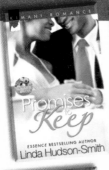

Your two books have a combined cover price of $13.98, but are yours **FREE!**

We'll even send you two wonderful surprise gifts. You can't lose!

THE EDITOR'S "THANK YOU" FREE GIFTS INCLUDE:

➤ Two Kimani™ Romance Novels
➤ Two exciting surprise gifts

YES! I have placed my Editor's "thank you" Free Gifts seal in the space provided at right. Please send me 2 FREE books, and my 2 FREE Mystery Gifts. I understand that I am under no obligation to purchase anything further, as explained on the back of this card.

PLACE FREE GIFTS SEAL HERE

About how many NEW paperback fiction books have you purchased in the past 3 months?

❏ 0-2   ❏ 3-6   ❏ 7 or more

E7XY   E5MH   E5MT

168/368 XDL

Please Print

FIRST NAME

LAST NAME

ADDRESS

APT.#   CITY

STATE/PROV.   ZIP/POSTAL CODE

Thank You!

Detach card and mail today. No stamp needed. ▶

© 2010 KIMANI PRESS. ® and ™ are trademarks owned and used by the trademark owner and/or its licensee. Printed in the U.S.A.

(K-ROM-10R2)

BUSINESS REPLY MAIL
FIRST-CLASS MAIL   PERMIT NO. 717   BUFFALO, NY

POSTAGE WILL BE PAID BY ADDRESSEE

THE READER SERVICE
PO BOX 1867
BUFFALO NY 14240-9952

NO POSTAGE
NECESSARY
IF MAILED
IN THE
UNITED STATES

God. That was exactly the kind of thing she should never hear.

Exactly the kind of thing she needed to hear.

There was no real way to lighten the mood or divert the conversation, but she felt she needed to point out the obvious. "You'll probably get sick of me in the next day or two, don't you think?" Funny how she said the words so easily when the mere possibility of this happening made her stomach drop; the chances of her getting tired of him anytime soon were somewhere between the probabilities of harvesting gold for food and spinning straw into usable petroleum. "We hardly know each other, Hunter."

"I know enough," he told her. "More than enough."

"Pick," Hunter said. "*A* or *B*."

After a delightful lunch on the terrace, he'd loaded her into his truck for the second half of what she was already thinking of as a fairy-tale day. Possibly the best day of her life, although she hated to make that concession before the sun even set on the horizon. Holding hands in a wonderful silence, they drove down a peaceful road with valley views of orange and gold in every direction. Now they'd come to a dead end, and Hunter, who seemed to be brimming with a kind of smug excitement, expected her to select the next activity.

"*B,*" she said, grinning and hoping she hadn't chosen between, say, a trip to either a mall or museum. Neither idea appealed to her. While she was here in Napa, she fully planned to spend as much time outside in the crisp air and sunshine as possible.

"*B* it is." Shooting her a return grin, Hunter turned right.

They drove a little farther and then, suddenly, the trees gave way to reveal flashes of startling color and—

"Balloons."

Clapping a hand over her frantically beating heart, she tried to keep some of her excitement inside lest they were planning to drive on past and head to an art museum after all. Four balloons, in various stages of inflatedness, stretched out in the valley before them, their baskets—gondolas, right?—waiting nearby. One was rainbow striped, one rainbow swirled and the other two were mostly blue with red zigzags. Did he know she'd always wanted to ride in one?

"Are we going on a balloon ride?"

Laughing, Hunter parked and cut the engine. "That's the plan. Unless you're scared of heights."

"Of *course* I'm scared of heights! Let's go!"

If she'd given herself more time to think about it, she'd have behaved with a little more decorum rather than leaping out of the truck and clapping and hopping like a two-year-old. She probably would have said her prayers and called her life insurance company to make sure she was paid up. But she was too excited and happy, and the sun was shining and she was free to play for once in her life.

Why not wallow in the joy?

"Thank you!" Racing around the truck's cab, she launched herself into Hunter's arms, nearly knocking him over with her Amazonian enthusiasm, poor guy. He was a good sport about it, laughing and holding her tight, and he didn't even protest when she planted sloppy kisses all over his face. "Thank you, thank you, *thank you!*"

"You're welcome, angel."

He set her back on her feet, staring at her with such glowing tenderness that she fully understood, deep in her gut, how much trouble she was in. This wasn't about having a bittersweet vacation fling and taking fond memories with her for the rest of her life. This was about falling crazy in love with a man who didn't belong in her world any more than she belonged in his. This was about her life changing into something unrecognizable, and if she was smart, she'd walk away now.

Instead, she held her hand out for his and they walked, together, to their balloon.

"We can sit here all night if we need to," Hunter said.

Kendra, who was sitting at the table with him, stared unhappily at her plate, which featured the healthy food selections they'd forced on her but no chicken nuggets, pizza or fries, and…wait for it…rolled her eyes at him. Again. For good measure, she clicked her tongue, too.

Down on the rug, his snout resting on his paws and his mournful brown eyes reflecting hope, Willard waited in utter stillness, clearly hoping that someone would drop a morsel of some kind on the floor.

Hunter had foolishly thought that he had at least a couple more years before being confronted with this kind of withering female attitude from his little girl, but he'd been wrong. The child was in a serious snit and would, any second, commence with the finger snapping and head bobbing.

Picking up a piece of asparagus with two fingers, she hung it upside down and eyed it the way she would a dead snake. "I'm not eating this."

After sneaking a quick peek at his watch—only six thirty-three, thank goodness, so he still had plenty of time to argue with the diva here and cook dinner for Livia—he shrugged.

"Suit yourself. But you're going to have a long and hungry night with no dessert if you choose not to eat it. And Grandma made peach ice cream."

He waited.

Folding her arms on the table (he waged an inner debate with himself but now was not the time to engage in an additional battle about elbows and manners), she regarded her plate with utmost gloom. After a shuddering sigh, she opened her mouth and took half a nip off the end of the asparagus, probably not enough for the vegetable's flavor to reach her taste buds.

"Eww." Scrunching her face, she stabbed a bite of salmon and let the fork hover one inch from her lips. "Why can't Livia eat with us again tonight?"

Mom sailed in through the patio doors just then and did a poor job of suppressing her smile of glee.

"Don't mind me," she said, not quite meeting his eye as she set the bushel of tomatoes she was carrying on the counter. She, along with Kendra, Dad and Willard, all seemed to bitterly resent his commandeering Livia for his own tonight and were unlikely to forgive his selfishness anytime soon. Mom, in fact, was only too happy to watch him squirm on Kendra's hot seat for a little while. "I don't want to interrupt."

"Why?" Kendra demanded again.

"Well," he said, reaching deep for his patience and finding none, "as I've already explained forty or fifty times, Livia and I are having dinner alone together in a little while. So you can see her another time. And it's not like you haven't seen her today. Didn't she stop by the doghouse—"

"Dragon's den," the girl corrected.

"—earlier?"

"But why can't I have dinner with you?"

"Because then Livia and I wouldn't be having dinner alone, would we?"

This logic didn't come close to piercing Kendra's intransigence. Lifting her head up again, brimming with the spirit of peaceful compromise, she decided to sweeten the deal.

"But I can be quiet. Really quiet."

Hunter snorted. "What, quiet like you were at last night's dinner? With your nonstop yakking about dinosaurs? No, thank you."

Willard, who seemed to have grown tired of the passive approach to food acquisition, sat up on his haunches, rested the very tip of his nose on the table, one inch from Kendra's plate, and snuffled at the salmon.

Kendra looked affronted with Hunter, her little brows flattening with the implication that her two-hour monologue on all things dinosaur had been anything less than scintillating. "Livia loves dinosaurs like I do. And I need to show her my shirt."

She pointed to today's model, a white one featuring a snarling tyrannosaur and the caption I'm a T. rex Trapped in a Human's Body.

"She saw it earlier," Hunter reminded her.

"But she really liked it. It made her laugh."

While he understood the idea of people becoming addicted to Livia's laughter, especially since he was confronting this issue himself, there was no way he was going to bring his six-year-old along on the romantic date night he had planned. Wouldn't happen, not even for a million tax-free dollars.

"Sorry, Charlie."

"But why-yyy-yyy?" Kendra whined, producing a remarkable number of syllables out of those three letters.

Grappling for the right words, which were nowhere in sight, Hunter made the mistake of looking up and catching Mom's eye. She winked, a tiny gesture that told him she understood his turmoil even if Kendra never would.

Why couldn't Kendra come?

One: because he was a greedy bastard and wanted Livia all to himself tonight.

Two: because he didn't want his daughter getting too attached to a woman who'd be gone from their lives all too soon.

He was a grown man; he knew what he was getting into. Well, no, he didn't. Not with Livia, not really. But he was a grown man and he knew about consequences and knew he'd chosen to deal with them, painful as they'd inevitably be when Livia went back to her real world and left him here in his.

But Kendra was a six-year-old who'd already lost both her mother and most of her words for a long time after. Her emotions were not in play here and never would be if he had anything to say about it, and he did.

Protecting this precious child from further heartbreak was his sacred duty as her father and he didn't plan to fall down on this job. Wasn't making hard decisions for the greater good in his job description? Kendra may not like it, but she didn't get a vote on the issue any more than she got a vote about whether she needed her vaccinations or not.

Kendra could spend time with Livia, in small, controlled doses, where Livia wouldn't have the opportunity to ingratiate herself into Kendra's routine too much and the chances of the girl falling in love with her were remote.

His plan was to guard his daughter's affections and he needed to stick to it, no matter how difficult it might be. And it would be very difficult because his beautiful supermodel—when had he begun thinking of Livia as his?—had a way of enchanting those around her without even trying.

So he stared into the hopeful face of a child who was starved for a mother figure and gently told her the painful truth, "We can't expect Livia to be around here too much, okay? She's going home soon, and we won't be able to see her anymore after that because she lives so far away."

Kendra stared at him in uncomprehending silence for two of the longest beats of his life. And then, her face twisting with bitter disappointment, she shoved her plate across the table and slumped her forehead on her arms.

Beside her, Willard whined in sympathy and rested his head on her knee.

Chapter 9

"Are we almost there yet? I can see lights."

Livia and Hunter turned a corner on the stone path and she tugged his hand a little harder. They both had long-legged strides but he was moving way too slowly for her tastes right now, and she couldn't wait to see what additional wonders this day held for them. He'd met her at the cottage just as the sun was setting, walked her down this lovely path—everything in Napa seemed to be lovely; apparently the region had received more than its fair share of beautiful spots when God was handing them out—and kept up a sphinxlike silence about his plans for their dinner.

Aaaand…he still wasn't talking.

As though he knew it would make her explode with impatience, he laughed and shrugged with smug satisfaction rather than answer her question. Luckily for him, the trees gave way at that point, revealing a beautiful setting and sparing him from a sharp smack on the arm.

"Oh, wow, what a pretty house!" she cried. "Is that yours?"

"It's mine."

Mission-style, with the typical white stucco and red tiled roof, the small house sat tucked into the hillside. Everything about it was beautiful and welcoming, from the overflowing flowerpots to the drapes fluttering in the open cloverleaf-shaped windows and the warm glow of lamps from inside. Even the air around here smelled good, like grilled steaks and vegetables or something, and, if she wasn't mistaken, the homey crispness of wood smoke.

She headed for the front door, propelled by her unreasonable curiosity about All Things Hunter and dying to see what kind of furniture he had, but he steered her around back.

"This way," he said, grinning.

That smile of his distracted her, the way it always did. All dimples and boyish delight, it was a thing of wonder that should be marked on tourist maps as a not-to-be-missed local sight.

"You have the sexiest smile," she blurted. *Way to throw yourself at the man, girl. Mama would be so proud.* "I can't believe I ever thought you were the world's grumpiest man."

He changed in an instant, the amusement vanishing in favor of dark desires and naked heat. "Is that so?"

"Oh, yeah."

"Are you trying to seduce me?"

"Is it working?"

"It's working." Leaning in, he gave her a nipping little kiss that began with the tip of his tongue and ended with a gentle tug of her bottom lip. She gasped with a sudden, twisting need that felt like a living thing inside her and fought the urge to reach for him, to bring him close. "You have no idea how well it's working. But I promised you dinner, didn't I? Come on."

Dinner had just dropped to number nine-hundred-eighty-five on her to-do list, but it seemed polite to show some interest since he'd gone to a lot of trouble. So she let him lead her around the path, which was lit with white lights strung through the bushes, to the back of the house.

Where the most amazing wonderland awaited her.

"Oh." Multisyllabic words failed her. *"Wow."*

"You like?"

"I *love.*"

What wasn't there to love? Beautiful potted trees and flowers—a man who grew things for a living had to have a spectacular yard, right?—wove their way down a lush green hill that ended in a wooden dock and, beyond that, a rippling pond. A trick of the moonlight (or maybe it was the glowing white Japanese lanterns he'd strung overhead that did it) made white spots shimmer on the water, creating an effect like diamonds sparkling over satin.

The dock seemed to be their ultimate destination for the night, because it was edged and illuminated by several flickering column candles and a domed fire pit that crackled merrily. Inside the ring of light was a spread blanket, a wicker basket and a champagne bucket.

And people said you had to die to reach paradise.

Who knew?

Emotion gathered in her throat, requiring her to clear it once or twice. It wasn't that men never tried to impress her with romantic gestures; they did. All the time, in fact. It was that it was meaningless if some rapper had his personal assistant order her a ruby bracelet while also ordering emerald and sapphire ones for the other models he had his eye on.

This simple picnic meant more to her than anything had since…

Since…ever?

Was that giving him too much credit? Or had her life, and the people inhabiting it, simply become that shallow and meaningless over the years?

"Is this all for me?" She swiped at her tears, hoping he wouldn't notice if she started bawling like Kendra probably did at bedtime.

He widened his eyes with fake shock and dismay. "Is that what you…? Oh, man, this is awkward. This is for my real date, who's due any minute. I was just hoping you'd tell me if you thought she'd like it."

"Stop it!" Laughing now and feeling like a complete idiot, she smacked him on the arm. "You know what I mean."

"Of course it's for you."

"This is a lot of effort," she pointed out.

"You're worth it."

That disarming honesty of his really did a number on her. Back in L.A., people practically gave themselves whiplash with their overenthusiastic and utterly insincere efforts to kiss her ass at every turn. All that was bull, and she knew it, but, hey, if it got her a nice table at a restaurant every now and then, well…so be it.

Hunter, on the other hand, seemed incapable of that kind of nonsense. The little bit she knew of him so far screamed that what she saw with him was what she got.

Wasn't that a refreshing change?

Taking a step closer, she decided to lay it all on the line. "Can I tell you something?"

He studied her for a few seconds, not answering, and that sizzling hyperawareness of him and his every reaction almost made her shiver, it was that acute. What did he see in her face when he looked at her so intently? Why couldn't she shake the certainty that he knew and understood things about her that she'd never suspected about herself? And why did that feel okay?

"You can tell me anything."

"You scare me to death," she said helplessly. "I'm almost shaking with it."

The edges of his eyes crinkled with the beginnings

of a smile, softening all those harsh planes and angles, making him tender but no less fierce.

"So that's it, then? We walk away?"

She tried to take a nice, deep breath to calm herself, but that swooping sensation remained in her belly, as though her little boat was bobbing along in the waves with no way to control the tide's sweep. If she was about to capsize and drown, she almost didn't care.

"That's the funny thing," she told him. "The thought of walking away scares me more than staying."

"Well, then." Touching her with a vibrating restraint, as though he only trusted himself on a very short leash, he smoothed a fluttering lock of her hair away from her face. "Stay."

Hunter led her to the dock, to the quilted picnic blanket, and stretched out on it, intending to lay her down with him. Livia had another, better, idea. With the light wind ruffling her hair and the firelight making her skin glow and giving her eyes a wickedly female glint, she arched her back and, in one fluid movement, pulled her sweater off over her head, dropping it to her feet. Holding his gaze, she unzipped her jeans and shimmied out of them, tossing those away, too, and revealing herself to him with a generosity and raw sensuality he could only have dreamed about.

Levering himself up on one elbow, he stared.

She was so freaking amazing in so many ways he could hardly wrap his brain around it. Long and lean, but curves—and plenty of them—everywhere that counted.

She wore a lacy black bra that cradled the perfect plump ovals of her breasts and revealed every detail to his searching eyes. Nipples, aroused and jutting, perfectly centered within dark areolae.

Belly that was fit and toned but still rounded and feminine, made all the more intriguing by the winking stone in her navel. Note to self: check that out at first opportunity.

Wide hips that would give him plenty to hang on to during the thrusting he planned to do, and skimpy little panties that did nothing to hide the bare cleft he intended to taste in the next three minutes. Strong thighs that he wanted up around his shoulders and then, later, wrapped around his waist in a death grip. Shapely legs, gleaming skin, knowing eyes, as though she fully comprehended that she'd just blown his mind and wasn't done with him yet.

Cracking open his dry mouth, he spoke in an urgent and guttural voice he barely recognized as his own. "Come here."

A slow grin, as lazy as it was dangerous, crept across her lips, heating his skin and tightening something inside him to the snapping point. Taking way too long about the whole process, she crouched and then dropped to all fours, crawling up the length of his body with a tiger's grace and a centerfold's in-your-face sexuality.

Thank God she wasn't shy; there were too many things he wanted to do to and with her, too much ground they had to cover while she was here. If he had to hold himself back long enough to bring her out of a shell, he'd suffer cardiac arrest and then spontaneous combustion.

No. This was a woman who knew how to give and, more importantly, to receive pleasure. Which was good because, while he'd planned a picnic for tonight and would've waited if she wasn't ready, this was what he'd wanted.

Exactly this.

When she was almost within range of his reaching hands, she paused, her face level with his groin. Then, flashing him a smoldering look that had his blood flowing as hot and thick as boiling honey, she nuzzled him with her cheeks, laughing a soft laugh of such wanton satisfaction that he hardened as though she'd already sucked him deep into her mouth.

Right about then, his head became too heavy to hold up and he let it fall back to the blanket and gathered fistfuls of her silky hair to hold her in place. Jesus. He hadn't known he could get this aroused from just the hint of a sex act, hadn't known he was still capable of the kind of desperate need that clawed at him from the inside out.

A drumbeat began, thudding in time with his pulse, and it felt so powerful that he was surprised it didn't echo all around the pond.

Livia…Livia…Livia.

Had he only known her for a few days? It felt like he'd waited a thousand lifetimes for this, and he couldn't get her close enough to stop that rising need from driving him wild. When she laughed again, reaching around to wedge her hands beneath him to squeeze his ass, something in his head snapped.

Letting go of her hair, he grabbed her shoulders and jerked her back. After a groaned protest, she raised her defiant and disgruntled gaze to his. They stared at each other for an arrested second, long enough for him to feel her frustrated restraint shudder through her.

"I need you," she said. "Now."

He couldn't control himself. Not when she played dirty like that. "You're playing with fire," he warned.

"Then burn me."

There went all of his fantasies of finessing her and being a gentle and considerate lover, up in a cloud of lust-induced smoke. In a burst of movement that he really hoped didn't scare the hell out of her, he reared up over her, grabbed her hips and unceremoniously pulled them out from under her, until she was flat on her back.

Impatience made him shake; he needed two tries to tug his sweater off over his head and three to unbutton his jeans and work the zipper over his straining erection.

It took her too long to unfasten the front of her bra, and she had no business doing that anyway when he was itching to touch her. So he caught both of her hands in one of his and pinned them to the blanket over her head, where they were out of his way.

"I'll do that," he said, undoing the clasp.

Wrong move. Because the sight of those breasts bouncing free, the nipples dark and distended and just begging for his mouth, brought out the poorly hidden animal in him. Growling—yeah, he actually made a crazy rumbling sound like a dog going for his bone and protecting it from the rest of his pack—he filled his hands to overflowing with all that firm flesh, squeezed them together, and tasted. Licking and suckling, rubbing and nipping, he hoped, in a distant corner of his overwrought mind, that she liked what he was doing because it sure as hell was working for him.

He couldn't get enough of all the sensations of her. Like the way when he drew hard on a nipple, using his tongue to stroke that sweet deliciousness against the roof of his mouth, her fingers tightened on his head, scratching his scalp in a desperate effort to keep him close. Or the way her back arched, making her rise up to meet him, and her strangled cries coalesced into a symphony of all the things he wanted to hear.

"Hunter…ah, God, don't stop. Don't stop…*please*."

She was everything. In the entire world, there was only her body in his hands, her voice in his ears, her taste in his mouth and the faint and earthy scent of her arousal filling his nostrils. She was everything, and he couldn't get enough.

Thrilling as these breasts were, he had other ground to cover.

Sliding lower, he rubbed his face all over her heaving belly, encountering that tiny little ring he'd seen earlier. Interesting. Wonder what she'd do if he dipped his tongue—

"Hunter." She writhed, her hips twisting and apparently beyond her control. *"Hunter."*

Oh, yeah. He liked that.

And he liked those sexy little panties but they had to go, and he didn't have time for sliding them down her ten miles of legs. What else could he do? Using both hands, he ripped them apart, pulled them off and threw them…somewhere.

There she was. That beautiful cleft between her thighs was swollen and ruddy, glistening with cream that he needed to taste. Leaning down—man, he was about to explode here—he breathed her in, making himself high with her scent, and then he ran his tongue over her with the kind of greed that would be right at home at an all-night buffet. Above him, she'd gone silent, either too stunned by this raw pleasure between them to speak—or asleep.

He was betting she wasn't asleep.

"Stop torturing me." Her breathless voice was the tiniest whisper, something he felt more than heard. "I need you inside me."

Yeah. He needed that, too.

Shoving his jeans and boxer briefs just far enough down his hips to free himself, he rose up, hooking her behind the knee with the crook of his arm and spreading her wide as he went. There was a second as he looked into her face and saw the stars' reflection in her heavy-lidded eyes and those dewy lips of hers, swollen now, curled in a half smile, that he absolutely couldn't breathe. Poised to enter all that slick heat, he felt something swell inside him that had nothing to do with the orgasm gathering strength and getting ready to let loose.

Had he done something right? Was that it? Because

he'd never imagined he had an experience like this—a woman like this—coming to him.

"Livia," he said, but beyond that he was mute.

Her answer was to widen that smile by an inch, tip her chin up and give his bottom lip a long, slow stroke with her tongue.

Anything he'd been holding back from her was unleashed by that single act.

Groaning, he palmed the engorged length of his penis and entered her with a single hard thrust.

Chapter 10

Jesus.

The feeling of all that honey-slick tightness closing around him almost stroked him out on the spot. Paralyzed with exquisite sensation, he didn't dare move below the waist but couldn't stop his eyes from rolling closed or his head from dropping into the fragrant hollow between her neck and shoulder. She smelled like honeysuckle and felt like an unspeakable new heaven that he hadn't had to die to reach. This fitting together of their bodies also felt like home.

Never in his life, not ever once, had being with a woman unraveled him like this.

Moving against him, she circled her hips and moaned with such unabashed delight that she snapped him out of it and fired him up even more, if that were possible.

Pulling out to the tip, he thrust, setting a punishing pace that made him both lose his mind and also settle more fully into her body than he'd been before.

Those long legs of hers wrapped around him with the strength of a vise grip and he went deeper. Felt more.

Every detail came into excruciating focus: the cool night air against his back, the candlelight surrounding them, the slapping contact of his tightening balls and her ass, her flattened breasts against his chest, the hard twin points of her nipples, the silk of her hair in his hands, the wet fullness of her sucking tongue in his mouth and the encouraging croon in her throat.

It was all too much; he wouldn't have been able to hold anything back even if the punishment was death.

Just as her cries reached a thrilling crescendo and her inner muscles began their rhythmic pulse around him, the orgasm roared through him with the force of an arrow shooting out of an Olympic archer's bow.

He came. And came and came and came, shouting her name and pouring so much of himself inside her that he had no hope of ever being whole without her ever again. The whole time they rode it out, he gathered her closer, held her tighter, and even when his body's urgency had begun to cool and it should have been enough, it wasn't.

They melted together into the blanket, still joined, and the kissing subsided into nuzzles until, finally, he shifted enough of his weight for her to breathe and rested his forehead against her cheek.

When sated exhaustion should have been claiming

him, his thoughts danced to life and twirled through his brain as though someone was throwing an impromptu party with four hundred dancing couples in there.

Wait a minute…what the hell just happened?

He hadn't finessed her.

He hadn't managed to take his jeans and underwear all the way off and was now hobbled about the ankles like some unfortunate horse.

He hadn't remembered to use a condom.

None of that particularly bothered him. In fact, he couldn't wait to do it again.

That was what bothered him.

What had happened to his life since this sweet siren showed up in it? What was she doing to him? What the hell was he going to do when she left?

Apprehension shivered through him, making him cold.

"What's wrong?" she asked.

He lifted his lids to see those clear hazel eyes staring into his, waiting for an answer he couldn't provide. What could he say? That he had the growing fear that he couldn't live without her? That he hadn't thought about his dead wife Annette during this interlude, not even once? That the more time he spent with Livia, the more living he wanted to do, even though he'd spent years wishing the accident had killed him, too? That this thing between them was so much bigger than he'd anticipated?

Of course not.

"I meant to use a condom," he said instead. "I'm sorry."

"We'll use them next time. I'm on the pill anyway."

"Yeah?" he said, trying to act like this was good news when his gut was doing a sickening little lurch.

"So." Turning her head, she ran the backs of her fingers against his cheek and kissed him again, slipping her tongue into his mouth, where he wanted it. "Should we eat some of that dinner you cooked?"

"Yeah," he said, rolling over her again and giving those spectacular breasts a bit more of the attention they deserved. "In a minute."

Hunter walked her back to her cottage just as a pink-tinged dawn was breaking against the mountains on the horizon. What was that saying? Oh, yeah—Red in the morning, sailors take warning; red at night is sailors' delight. Or something like that. So that meant rain today, for the first time since she'd arrived. She could already touch the growing damp in the breeze and it felt like an omen worth noting.

Something had changed. Sometime between their glorious night on the dock, huddled under the quilts, making love, talking and eating the world's best grilled steaks, the walk to the cottage and now, Hunter had stopped touching her. For good measure, he'd even shoved his hands into his jeans pockets and had them balled into unmistakable fists.

That was bad.

What was worse was his shifting gaze, which seemed

to land on everything that wasn't her. The growing awkwardness between them felt like approaching doom, and if she'd looked up to see a rampaging herd of elephants heading in their direction, she'd have this same suffocating tightness in her throat.

Still, she didn't have to act needy. For one, Mama didn't raise any fools, and for two, he'd never promised her a lifetime, or even more than one night, of that heart-stopping sex.

He was a man, she was a woman, they'd enjoyed each other and maybe now it was over. Fine. Big deal. She was a grown woman and she'd get over it without lowering herself to the level of burrs clinging to his pants as he walked.

Her? Please. She was so far above all that kind of nonsense it wasn't even funny. Many people considered her to be one of the most beautiful women in the world, so she didn't need to fret and wonder about any particular man. Someone else would turn up soon.

What was it that Beyoncé sang? "I can have another you by tomorrow," wasn't it? Yeah. That.

Opening her mouth, she prepared to say something witty and unconcerned so she could demonstrate her sophisticated understanding of what sex meant and didn't mean.

"Will I see you later?" she blurted.

At last he looked at her and she wished he hadn't. Gone was her lover from last night, replaced by the cool-eyed, granite-faced stranger who'd confronted her in the parking lot that first day. This was the man she didn't know and wasn't sure she wanted to know.

As though he knew something was going on and she needed moral support from wherever she could find it, Willard materialized just then, providing a much needed, though temporary, distraction. Yawning and shaking that huge body to wake himself all the way up, he woofed, trotted over and sat at her feet, bumping her hand with his head in case she needed a hint.

Grateful for his comfort, she scratched his ears and clung to his warmth, since she wasn't getting any from Hunter, who ignored her question altogether.

"When are you leaving?" he asked.

Ah. Was that the heart of the matter, then? Did he prefer she pack and head out right now or was the thought of her going home killing him? Looked like the former.

"Ethan and Rachel are due this evening. We'll check out the chapel, I guess, and then head out as early as tomorrow."

"Tomorrow," he echoed.

His face gave nothing away, which was a real trick. Though she'd done a little acting, she wasn't good enough to stand here and play it cool for another second, so it was time to wrap this up.

Forcing a smile, she kept her voice light. "Thanks for the picnic."

There went his gaze again, shifting off toward something over her shoulder while he jerked his thumb over his own. "I should get going. Kendra'll be getting ready for school soon, and I need to—"

"I understand," she said quickly, beginning to hate him with a seething virulence that they should really bottle and use as a pesticide, it was that strong.

He nodded, already a thousand miles away from her before his steps took him to the edge of the porch. There was no kiss. No hug. Nothing but the generic "See you later" that he might've said to the cashier at the farmer's market.

"See you later," she replied.

She watched him go as the first drops of rain began to fall.

The rain came down in driving sheets that did nothing to help Livia's gloomy mood. Going out in that mess was unthinkable so she never even considered it. After showering and a room service breakfast, she took up a listless post on the living room sofa, watching a *Dog Wrangler* marathon (the episode with the bulldog's obsession with skateboarding always made her laugh) on the B and B's satellite TV system and hunkering under a down blanket for comfort.

Willard, who'd apparently decided he was her pet, sprawled atop her legs, which was something like cuddling with an overweight fawn. To her surprise, he was a fine companion, except for when he barked back at the barking dogs on the show. That, she could do without.

Hunter didn't call.

Not during the morning and not after she shared her paella lunch with Willard, who loved the shrimp but wasn't so big on the mussels. When three o'clock-ish came, she figured he was getting Kendra off the bus from school, and when four o'clock came, she wondered if she should maybe think about changing her clothes for when Ethan and Rachel arrived.

Buuuut…nah.

It was so much better to wallow in her self-pity for being stupid enough to fall more than halfway in love with a man she'd met on vacation.

The loneliness was excruciating, which was pretty funny considering she'd only known him for a few days. If she'd never met him, she'd've been fine. If she'd merely kissed and flirted with him, she'd've been fine. Hell, if she'd merely had sex with him, she probably would've been fine.

But the agonizing combination of their wonderful daytime hours yesterday followed by the best sex of her life, followed by snuggling and talking and more sex, followed by today's absolute absence of him from her life, made her feel as though she was dying. As though the best part of her had been ripped away and wasn't coming back. As though this echoing hollowness inside her could never be filled.

How crazy was that?

She levered herself up just enough to gaze down at the dog, who had his snout resting on her knees. "Am I insane, Willard?"

That mournful look of his was answer enough.

Yeah. It figured.

Slumping back with emotional exhaustion, she tried to refocus on TV.

Screw Hunter Chambers. *Screw him.*

Her cell phone bleated, the sound echoing off the walls like the crack of a rifle. First she jumped ten feet in the air. Then her pulse went haywire on account of her soaring heart. Then she scrambled upright and grabbed it off the end table, simultaneously smoothing her Medusa-worthy hair out of her face, like *that* mattered.

True, she'd written Hunter off and never wanted to see him again. But that didn't mean she wouldn't take his call and read him the riot act for this shabby treatment today. Oh, yes. If he thought he could do this to her, then he'd better— "Hello?"

"Hey, girl," said Rachel.

"Oh." It was impossible to switch gears between crashing disappointment that it wasn't Hunter and happy surprise that it was Rachel instead, so she didn't even try. "Rachel. Hi."

"Okay, what's wrong with you? Did you get hit by a truck?"

Friends. That was both the good thing and the bad thing about them—they knew when you were feeling down in the dumps and didn't have the decency to ignore your misery and let you wallow in peace. Normally she told Rachel everything that was going on, but then she'd never had her life turned upside down quite the way Hunter had done. Now wasn't the time to get into it; she'd barely had time to process anything herself, and there'd be time enough to dissect her tragic love life once Rachel and Ethan arrived.

"Hello?" Rachel snapped. "What's wrong?"

"Cramps," Livia lied. "Are you on your way?"

"Ah. About that..."

"No way. No. Freaking. Way."

"We can't get away yet, Livie. Sorry. This thing is running long and I—"

"Well, are you talking another day or two delay or—"

"Three weeks."

What? Three—*what?*

Dropping the phone away from her ear, Livia gaped at Willard, who yawned and scratched his jaw with one of his hind legs in an underwhelming display of support.

Okay. Okay, girl. Pull it together.

"Did you just say three weeks, Rachel? Is that what I'm hearing?"

"I'm sorry. I'm really, really sorry. But there's nothing we can do. This thing is so far behind schedule—"

"I'll just come home." Yeah. That made the most sense. "I'll come home tomorrow, and you and Ethan can come on your own, when you have time. You don't need me to scope locations for your wedding."

"No! I need you, and I was looking forward to this! You can't let me down like this—"

"I can't stay here for three more weeks." A desperate, lonely vista opened up before her at the idea: twenty-one days spent on this very sofa with Willard, longing for Hunter and remembering the good old day—yes, it'd only been one day, hadn't it?—when he'd pretended she meant something to him. She and Willard could order pizza. They could have joint massages and manicures. It'd be great.

Not.

"Yeah," she said, the decision made. "I'll come home. I'll get the first flight I can."

"Well, at least stay a couple more days. I thought you had all that sightseeing to do, and it's been so long since you had a vacation."

"Yeah. I don't think so."

Rachel heaved a big sigh and Livia could practically see her deflating over the phone. "Did you have a chance to meet Ethan's family?"

"I did."

"Well, don't keep me in suspense. What were his parents like? I've only talked to them on the phone so far. I can't wait to meet them."

A sudden stab of jealousy, her first ever toward Rachel, hit her. Soon Rachel would have those wonderful people for in-laws. Soon Rachel could call this vineyard home. Soon Rachel would belong here, with this family, and Livia never would.

"They were great. You'll love them."

"And what about Hunter? What's he like?"

Hunter.

Even the sound of his name hurt right now.

"He's a great guy," Livia said, fighting a mighty battle to keep her voice even and her sudden tears from falling.

Blinking furiously, she got control of herself, but only just. "You'll love him."

I love him.

The words were right there on the tip of her tongue, waiting to be said, but she bit them back. Love. She couldn't be in love with a man she'd only known for a few days. That was impossible. Ridiculous. Over-the-top romantic nonsense.

Wasn't it?

"What's he like?"

Lord almighty—what was with the questions? She was coming out of her skin here and Rachel wanted Hunter's personality profile? Was this a cosmic joke on her?

"I don't know, Rach," she said, the strain breaking through in her voice. "You'll have to see for your-self—"

Someone knocked at her door and her heart, foolish to the point of recklessness, leapt with renewed excitement and hope like a tongue-dangling retriever going after a ball.

Hunter? Was that Hunter? Did he care about her after all? Hunter? *Hunter?*

Pathetic.

"Hey, Rach," she said, already leaping from the sofa and making another futile effort to smooth her hair as she raced for the front door. "Someone's here. I gotta go, okay? Call you back."

"But—" Rachel spluttered.

Livia clicked the phone off and tossed it back on the

side table as she went past. Slowing down on the last couple of steps, she swung the door open and held her breath as—

"Kendra," she cried. "What're you doing here?"

The girl looked up at her, those big brown eyes filled with tragic despair, her chin trembling. Today she wore a green Future Paleontologist T-shirt with her shorts and carried a small square makeup suitcase circa 1960 or earlier in her hand. When Willard raced over to greet her, she patted his neck and gave his furry face a lingering kiss. Then she looked up at Livia, gathered all her courage around her with one dramatic breath and spoke in a heartbroken voice that would do a blues singer proud.

"Can I come in?" she asked.

"What are you doing here?" Livia asked again.

"I ran away."

"Oh," Livia said, trying not to laugh at this solemn moment. "Is that why you have the suitcase?"

"Yeah."

"What's in there, anyway?"

"My dragons and dinosaurs. Oh, and I packed a granola bar in case I got hungry, but I ate it already."

This child was too precious for words. "What about a change of clothes, underwear, a toothbrush and some money?"

Kendra's face fell. "I forgot those."

"I see."

Apparently tired of waiting for permission, she edged

past Livia and headed into the living room, making herself at home on the sofa. There was nothing for Livia to do but shut the door, follow her and sit on the coffee table facing her. Willard, who wouldn't let his pack go anywhere without him, trotted along and settled at their feet.

"What happened?"

"Daddy was mean to me."

"Oh, no."

"He yelled at me. And he wouldn't let me come see you."

Oh, really? Wasn't that interesting?

"Well," Livia said carefully, knowing it wasn't cool to interrogate a six-year-old, "Daddies yell sometimes. Did you not clean your room, or—"

"No." Kendra's voice was adamant, her outrage absolute. "He was grouchy when I got home from school. I didn't do *anything*. Even Grandma said he needed to get his act together or leave her kitchen."

Livia gaped at her, overwhelming hope making her head spin. "What do you think was wrong with him?"

Kendra shrugged, looking bewildered and victimized. "And then," she said with the rising excitement that told Livia she was getting to the juicy stuff, her father's worst offense against her, "I asked if I could come see you, and he yelled at me and shook his finger and said—" Kendra puffed herself up, wagged her finger and deepened her voice in a remarkably good imitation of Hunter "'—Miss Livia is on vacation and she'll be leaving tomorrow, so there's no point getting too attached to her!' And then he marched out and slammed the door! Really hard!"

"Hunter slammed the door?" Livia tried to get her mind around the image of Mr. Calm, Cool and Collected having a meltdown, but it was as incomprehensible as a hippopotamus being a principal dancer in *Swan Lake.* "Maybe he's just, you know, having a bad day, honey. I'm sure he didn't mean it."

"I can't live like that!"

"Ah…" Livia kept her lips pressed tightly together, fighting that urge to laugh again, because Kendra was clearly embracing her inner diva with this dramatic performance. "You can't just run away when—"

Moving in for the kill, Kendra hopped down from the sofa and scrambled into Livia's lap, where her solid weight and fruity-fresh little girl's fragrance were much too wonderful for Livia's overwrought nerves. Livia tried to brace herself against all this cuteness but that was no use, especially when Willard, who hated to be excluded from any nearby affection, rose up, rested his snout in the girl's lap and gave them both the soulful eye.

"Can I live here with you, Miss Livia?" Kendra begged. "Pleeeeeeeaaaaase?"

Allowing herself one precious minute of fantasies, Livia hugged her and kissed her fat cheeks. Both of them. What would it be like to have a child like this in her life, playing and giggling, whining and just sitting, like this, in quiet moments that were only special because they were together? What would it be like to tuck an angel like this into bed and wake up to her bleary smile in the mornings? What would she give to have a family of her own, with a husband and a child and a home that was really a home and not just the place where she landed in between shoots all over the world?

Would a million dollars cover it? Done. Ten million? No problem. And if her career interfered with the proper raising of a bright girl like this, the career would have to go, no question. Much as she'd worked and bled to get where she was right now, one of the top models in the world, she was coming to a painful realization that she should have known all along, just like Dorothy should've known there was no place like home.

Money didn't do you a damn bit of good when you had a yawning ache inside you that only a family of your own could fill.

But she didn't have a family of her own and this child, meanwhile, was waiting for an answer. So she gave Kendra's forehead a kiss, because she'd missed it on the first round of kisses, swallowed the growing tightness in her throat and gave the kind of understanding but regretful smile she imagined a good mother would give in this kind of situation.

"You can't live here with me, honey—"

"Pleeeeeeeaaaaase?" Kendra clasped her hands together, ramping up the enthusiasm. "I promise I'll—"

Livia held up a finger to silence her. "But…" she said.

Kendra snapped her jaws shut.

"If you're finished begging and whining…"

Kendra nodded violently.

"Then you can call your grandma to tell her where you are and apologize for scaring her, because I'm sure she's wondering if you've been kidnapped or eaten by cougars or something."

More nodding.

"And we can have snacks and give each other pedicures with this pretty pink polish I brought with me. How would that be?"

"Great! Thank you! Thank you–thank you–*thank you!*"

"Here's the phone."

Livia watched her dial and then chatter with her grandmother, certain that when she left Napa tomorrow, she'd be leaving a big chunk of her heart right here with Kendra.

The rain was relentless, pounding against Livia's windows until late in the evening and doing nothing to lift her spirits.

After the impromptu but delightful pedicures with Kendra, she'd walked her and Willard back to the big house and then, thoroughly sick of her own company and disgusted with her pity party of one, which had gone on long enough, she bundled up, had a quick sandwich at the winery's bistro (no sign of any of the Chambers family, thank goodness) and came back to finish her Jackie Robinson biography, which was excellent.

The Dog Wrangler marathon was still on at that point (they were now up to the episode with the nonretrieving golden retriever, a canine who also didn't know he could swim), so she watched it for a while and then decided to call it a night at eleven-thirty. She was making a last lap around the cottage, clicking off the lamps, when someone knocked on the door.

Hunter.

It was him; no one else would disturb her at this hour, not unless it was the local authorities trying to evacuate everyone at the winery on account of a pending flood or mud slide. Indecision nailed her feet to the floor while an excited hope made her lungs heave like giant bellows.

Her brain was just pissed.

Recovering just as the second round of knocks began, she marched through the foyer and flung the door open for the simple pleasure of telling him to go to hell. But then their gazes connected and her thoughts scattered like rioters being fire hosed.

The overhead porch light was bright enough for her to see that he looked drowned-rat terrible. His clothes and jacket were soaked, and the idiot didn't even have the sense to wear the baseball hat he'd had glued to his head the other day. Rivulets of rain ran down his forehead and dripped into eyes that were flashing dark and ferocious but otherwise unreadable. His jaw was tight, his lips thin. And she was so relieved, so unbelievably and unspeakably happy to see him after today's long hours without him, that it absolutely infuriated her.

He was the jerk, yeah, but she was the fool.

"Livia," he began.

She slammed the door in his face.

Better to cool off and deal with him later—or never—than risk letting him see what he'd done to her today and how she'd unraveled at the loss of his attention after their glorious night together. He'd either come because his guilty conscience was forcing him to put a nice period at the end of their little fling—his parents were decent folks, after all, and they'd probably taught him to treat women the way he'd want to be treated—or he'd come to stammer out some lame excuse in the hopes that he could have a no-strings-attached booty call.

Either way, it wasn't happening.

A sharp curse came from the other side of the door, and then pounding. "Livia," he said, and the husky aggravation in his voice made her want to break into a few joyous steps of the Electric Slide. "We need to talk. *Please.*"

She flicked off the porch light and bolted the door.

Is that a clear enough message for you, Hunter?

Filled with a savage satisfaction, she dusted off her hands—*buh-bye, jackass!*—took her time about folding the throw and draping it over the sofa's arm and turned off the last couple of living room lights before heading down the hall.

So he thought he could just play her, did he? Thought he could rock her world last night, kiss her off this morning, ignore her all day and then reappear tonight to a warm reception and her open legs?

No way, buddy. No. Freaking. Way.

She swept her sweater off over her head, thinking maybe she needed a shower to decompress before bed.

The steam would help soothe her raw nerves and the water—

"Oh, my God," she shrieked, backing into the nearest wall with a thunk.

Hunter stood in the middle of the bedroom, looking grim.

Chapter 11

A tense second passed, during which Livia tried to catch her breath and settle back into her skin. She opened her mouth to demand to know how he'd gotten in there, but the open window and displaced screen behind the fluttering curtains said it all so she snapped her jaws shut.

Who'd've thought her love of Napa's cool nighttime air would bite her in the ass in such a big way?

Since she hated being outflanked and outmaneuvered, she let both her temper and her sweater fly, hurling the latter at him. Naturally he deflected it with a casual swipe of his arm, the bastard.

"Don't scare me like that, you son of a—"

"Kindly don't slam the door in my face again."

That quiet calm of his was more than she could

take at the end of this long day of feeling abandoned and strung out. "Are we talking about manners here? Because I don't take kindly to being blown off, and I don't do booty calls. So you can get out right now."

"That's not why I'm here."

Too late she regretted the rashness of throwing her sweater at him, which left her both half-naked and vulnerable to the quiet pain in his eyes. It was more than that, actually. Those harsh facial lines, tight lips and the flashing brown turbulence all added up to one thing.

He'd spent his day every bit as tormented as she had.

That mattered to her but that didn't mean she was a marshmallow.

"What do you want?" she demanded, crossing her arms over her lacy white bra and praying he couldn't see the way her breasts swelled and her nipples tightened for him or the goose bumps rising all over her skin.

"Thanks for taking care of Kendra earlier."

"My pleasure."

"I hope she wasn't too much trouble."

"She was no trouble. I'm crazy about her."

"We're crazy about you."

Whoa. Something shifted just then, charging the air with enough electricity to power the Vegas strip for a month or so. She told herself that physical chemistry didn't amount to much, that keeping this roller-coaster ride going with him would lead to inevitable heartbreak for her, but none of that mattered when her skin was starved for his.

"*'We?'*" she echoed.

"*I*," he said softly. "*I* am crazy about you."

That raw ache in his voice went a long way toward soothing her bruised feelings and reassuring her. It was terrifying to fall, yeah, but how bad could it be if they both fell together? And he was falling, even if he didn't say it. She had eyes; she could see his fear.

Still. A reminder of recent events seemed like a good idea. "You didn't seem that crazy about me this morning. You couldn't leave me fast enough."

"This morning it was all I could do to remember that I have grapes to harvest and a winery to run." He swallowed hard, making his Adam's apple dip in a rough bob, and then confessed something else that made her knees weaken and her heart pound. "It was all I could do not to lose it when you told me you're leaving tomorrow."

The words came before she could think about the wisdom of telling him. "I don't... I don't have to leave tomorrow. Rachel and Ethan have been delayed again—"

"How long?" he demanded urgently, cutting her off.

"Three weeks."

His face twisted, although whether it was with a sob or a grin, she couldn't quite tell at first. "Three weeks," he repeated, and he said it with the wonder of a man who'd been gifted with a room full of beer, pizza and a recliner parked in front of a theater-sized TV tuned to ESPN. "Three weeks."

Much as she wanted to fall into his arms right now, they had to get some things straight. She couldn't spend another day like this one. No one had died, true, but another day like this one just might kill her.

"You hurt me this morning," she told him.

He stepped closer, his voice dropping to a whisper. "And you're making me feel things that scare me to death."

"So why come back now?"

"I can't stay away from you," he said simply. "It's out of my control."

That did it. She was now, officially, in love with this man.

With a glad sob, she launched herself into his arms.

They came together hard and fast, with a grappling urgency that bordered on violence. Hunter caught her face between his hands and angled it way back, imprisoning her and using aggressive licks and nips to possess her mouth. She opened up for him, a flower unfolding her petals for her sun, sucking him deeper, needing him more, needing it all.

In this world full of frightening new feelings between them, this was the scariest: he had her. She couldn't seem to give herself over to him fast enough. Not her body, certainly, and not her heart, either. They were his. All of her growing whimpers and cries belonged to him, and her swelling breasts and weeping sex were his, too. Did he know that she'd never lost herself like this before? That his presence sparked a fever in her and his smile made her head light?

Could he see this terrible weakness in her?

The words came and kept coming because he'd unlocked a hidden mechanism that wouldn't let her hold things back from him; everything she had and was belonged to him and she gave it freely. It wasn't enough that her shaking hands shoved aside his jacket and dove under his sweater, hungry for the hot skin underneath. She had to narrate everything, paint him a picture and draw him a map.

"I missed you." It was hard to kiss him and talk at the same time, but she somehow made it work, brushing her lips against his and tasting him with her tongue even as she rubbed her breasts against his unyielding chest and raked her nails up his back. "I missed you so much. I couldn't breathe with it."

"I missed you, too." Beneath all that smooth skin, she felt the flex of his tightening muscles, the vibrations as he tried to hold himself in check. He ran his hands all over her torso, zeroing in on her breasts and freeing them from her bra with a flick of his fingers. "You were all I could think about. This was all I could think about."

Stooping just enough, he pressed her breasts together in his rough grip, circling her nipples with his thumbs and then licking, sucking and biting them with primitive abandon, as though he'd been given only thirty seconds to claim every part of them and the only thing that mattered was not missing a single millimeter.

"Hunter…God. Don't stop. Don't stop, Hunter. Hunter. *Hunter.*"

"Shhh. It's okay, baby. It's okay—"

"I needed you inside me. Don't you know that? I need you…I need you…I need you, Hunter. Stay with me, okay? Stay with me. Please. *Please.*"

Was that her voice sobbing like that? Chanting like that? Which of them was making that animalistic sound—part growl and part purr? Who was shaking worse?

Leaving her breasts, he focused in on her cargo pants, undoing the button and then yanking with both hands to separate the zipper and pull them off over her hips. They fell to her ankles and she had just enough time to kick them away before he planted his hands on her ass and hefted her up.

Apparently no one had ever told him that she was an Amazon, taller and heavier than a lot of men she knew, because he tightened her thighs around his waist and swung her around toward the bed. Through her heavy-lidded eyes, she had a quick glimpse of him staring up at her, his expression glazed and alight, his lips swollen and his forehead damp. Then he dipped his head again, latched on to a nipple and suckled with long, rhythmic pulls that shot electric jolts of pleasure to the depths of her belly and made her inner muscles clench.

Blinded with the sensation, she clung to his neck for dear life but let her eyes roll closed and her head fall back. The next thing she knew, he was lowering her to the cool sheets and resting her head on the pillow, and there was no world but this, nothing but him standing by the bed, squirming out of his jeans and boxers to reveal a heavy erection that she needed inside her right now.

Reaching for him, she spread her thighs and angled her hips. "Now." There she went with the chanting again. It would have been funny if the need wasn't suffocating her alive. "Now, Hunter. Please. Now."

His feverish gaze locked with hers, his movements choppy and uncoordinated, he fumbled with something in his pocket and produced a tiny package wrapped with green foil. Something in her overwrought mind protested as she watched him rip it open and roll it on. They'd used them last night after the first time, yeah, but it seemed unnatural to have anything between them even if it was the smart thing to do. Worse, the delay took too long and she needed him buried deep when this gathering eruption roared through her as it was threatening to do any second.

"Hunter," she began again.

"Turn over."

Scrambling to obey, she rose up on all fours; presenting him with the tiny white whale tail of her thong panties between her cheeks. Since she and shame had parted ways a while back, the second he laid his hands on her, she dipped her back into a *U,* making herself as open and accessible to him as humanly possible.

Just in case he needed a hint.

"Christ," he muttered, then crawled onto the bed behind her and sank his teeth deep into her rounded flesh.

"Oh, God."

Jerking her hips back and up against him, he pulled off her thong and stroked the swollen flesh between her legs in an excruciating caress that had more sobs collecting in her throat. A rumble of approval was her only warning before he thrust deep, stretching her beyond endurance and hitting a hidden spot inside her body that made stars spark in front of her eyes.

"Yes," she said with what was left of her voice. "More."

Sliding up over her, he surrounded her on all sides, giving notice for the record. Her back was his because he'd covered it with his chest. Her neck was his because he'd clamped it between his teeth, using that exquisitely sensitive spot to hold her in place. Her dangling breasts belonged to one of his exploring hands and her engorged sex belonged to the other.

He thrust sharp and deep, taking it all and demanding more, letting go of her neck only to bite her ear as he spoke. "Say my name."

Hey—if he wanted it, it was his. Everything was his.

"Hunter," she gasped.

He withdrew to the tip and surged again, harder. "Who do you belong to?"

"You."

"Huh?"

"You, Hunter. *You.*"

"Do you want it like this?"

Funny guy. Laughter began in her throat only to be choked off by another moan of pleasure. "You know I do."

"Harder?"

"God, yes," she said, but even as the words were coming out of her mouth, she wondered how she could take any more before her body disintegrated. "Yes."

His rhythm picked up until their bodies slapped together and she felt like a very wicked girl for being punished like this. Deliciously wicked. Breathless and triumphant, she let the pleasure fill her up until she laughed.

He growled in the most primitive kind of masculine warning but she could hear the amusement in his voice. "This is funny?"

"You feel so good."

"Yeah?"

"Oh, yeah."

"Are you going to come for me?"

"Maybe."

The teasing sealed her fate. Unleashing anything he'd been holding back, he thrust into her with sharp strokes, in and out, biting her neck again and pinching one of her nipples for good measure.

She flew apart, shouting her release with an abandon she'd never felt before. And just at the moment she needed his driving force between her thighs, prolonging the ecstasy, he stiffened to concrete and refused to move.

"Don't stop," she begged. "Please don't—"

"Are you going to come again for me, Livia?"

"Please don't stop—"

"You're not holding back on me, are you?"

As if she could. "No," she gasped. "Just a little more. I just need a little more."

"Good girl."

He surged again, harder and deeper, and she dissolved into spasms of such intense pleasure she didn't know how she could survive. She opened her mouth to let it out, but she had nothing left because he'd taken it all.

She collapsed into the pillows, sated and exhausted, and listened to his raw voice say her name in an endless stream as he drove into her, again and again, and then, with a hoarse shout, went rigid all around her.

When it was over, they stretched out, fitting together so well they could only have been made for each other, and she drifted toward peace and oblivion with his lips brushing back and forth against her nape.

"Do me a favor," he murmured just as she was falling asleep.

"Hmm?" Turning her head to receive his kiss on her cheek, she brought his hand to her breasts to make sure he didn't let her go during the night and settled her butt more firmly into his lap.

"Think about how we can see each other when your vacation is over."

Now this was worth staying awake for. Lifting her

heavy lids, she twisted her neck a little further so she'd be able to see his eyes. They were smiling. Intent. Happy. Knowing that she'd had something to do with putting a look like that on such a man's face was overwhelming. Incomprehensible.

"Yeah?"

He skimmed the corner of her lips with a featherlight kiss that made tension coil in her belly and heat pool— again!—between her legs. "Can you do that for me?"

Yes was the answer, but before she could give it, he slid his mouth a couple of inches in the right direction, beginning the dance all over again. As she turned in his arms and sucked his tongue deeper into her mouth, her last coherent thought was that they were going to have another deliciously sleepless night.

"Should we be doing this?" Livia asked, her voice hushed.

He had to grin. The woman who'd made a fine living displaying her body for the world to see was turning shy on him over a late dip in the B and B's spa. Was that funny or what? Despite the fact that it was two in the morning, the whole place was asleep and he'd only turned on a couple of discreet lights inside the fenced and landscaped area, Livia was bundled up tight in the white floor-length terry cloth robe he'd nabbed from the massage area for her. Looking worried, she watched him relax into the churning water and dipped one toe in.

"What if someone catches us?" she wondered.

Closing his eyes, he rested his arms on the ledge and

leaned his head back. Heaven. The hot water against the cool night air on his face (it had finally stopped raining) was absolute heaven. Well, no. Being buried inside Livia's body, making love to her—that was absolute heaven. This was…heaven's basement.

"If someone catches us, then we'll apologize and leave. In the meantime, I'm staying here until my skin wrinkles." He cracked one eye open. "You coming in or not?"

With a final, furtive glance in all directions, she unbelted the robe, slipped it off—yeah, he needed both eyes open for that—and slid into the spa and onto the bench beside him.

"Oh," she breathed, her eyes rolling closed and her head tipping back with exaggerated ecstasy. "*God.* Why didn't you tell me?"

"I tried. You didn't listen."

"Hmm."

They sat in silence for a minute, melting into the relaxing swirl, and he figured now was as good a time as any to bring up a subject that'd been nagging at his brain for a while now.

"Can I ask you something?"

"Course," she murmured.

He stared at her, wanting to see her reaction. "Why haven't you ever gotten married?"

Those hazel eyes opened and crinkled in a wry smile. "My life isn't exactly conducive to successful relationships, is it?"

Why did that simple truth sting so much? And why

did he feel this relentless compulsion to tiptoe down this road with her? "Why's that?"

"I'm always traveling, for one. For two, a lot of the men I meet are, ah—"

"Unworthy?" he supplied sourly, thinking of rumors he'd heard a while back about her dating some producer who'd later run off with an actress.

That made her grin. "*Unworthy.* I like that."

This should've been answer enough but it wasn't. "They can't all be unworthy."

"No," she agreed. "Some are intimidated. Some could be worthy but are more concerned with a trophy on their arms and don't bother to ever see me."

What did that mean? "*See* you?"

"Me." Lifting a hand out of the water, she touched it to her heart and he got it. "*Me.*"

For reasons that eluded him at the moment, this explanation made him unreasonably happy. Maybe it was because he wasn't rich or famous, didn't have his own jet and couldn't give her a part in a movie that would make her acting career.

But, unlike those other men, he saw her. Not just the outer shell—her.

He saw the fierce pride and the keen intelligence, the sweetness and the strength. He saw the beauty of her smile, yeah, but he also saw the greater beauty of her heart.

Did she know that? Should he tell her?

Covering her hand with his, he pressed it to her chest, where the water thrashed and her heart thudded. When her breath caught and her uncertain gaze flickered to his, he leaned in to give her lips a gentle but lingering kiss.

"I see you, Livia."

"Yeah?" she whispered.

"You're beautiful." Nudging her hand aside, he settled his fingers against the silky slickness of the valley between her bobbing breasts. "*This* is beautiful."

Because he didn't trust his voice to say anything further, not now, he slid his hands to the curve where waist met hips, pulled her around until she straddled his lap and showed her just how special he thought she was.

Chapter 12

"Hey, sexy."

Rolling the driver's-side window down a little farther, Hunter leaned his elbow on the door and steered the truck alongside Livia. She liked to ride her bike for an hour or so after lunch every day and, as luck would have it, he just happened to be traveling this very same road, on his way back from picking up a few things in town.

What a delightful coincidence. Or not.

Why burden the poor woman with the information that he was finding it increasingly difficult to make it through the long hours between when they left each other's beds in the mornings and their afternoon glass of wine together? Was there any reason to tell her he'd been driving up and down these roads for the past fifteen minutes, hoping to catch a glimpse of her? No way. God knew he'd already lost his head enough over her; there was no reason to confess it outright. What if she thought he was a stalker?

"You need a lift?"

Grinning, she hopped off the bike and stared over her shoulder at him, her eyes hidden and mysterious behind dark sunglasses. Along with her helmet, she wore those same sexy shorts from that day he ran her off the road, and, unbelievably, the same tank top, although she had another shirt of some type tied around her waist and apparently planned to use it when she got back to civilization. Pulling the glasses down to the tip of her nose, she gave him a once-over and pretended to give it serious thought.

"I don't know," she said. "Mama always told me to watch out for strange men."

"Honey," he said before he backed the truck under a tree just off the road, "if your mama knew the kinds of things I wanted to do with you, she'd call the police."

There it was again: that delighted and delightful laugh, the sunshine in his life that had nothing to do with the bright sky overhead. How this woman had worked her way this deep under his skin and into his blood in only a few short weeks was a mystery he really needed to figure out at some point.

If only he wasn't too whipped to think.

"I'm not sure." Taking her helmet and glasses off, she tipped her face up to his as he approached, revealing flushed skin that was dewy with sweat and musky with the best fragrance in the world—healthy woman. *This* healthy woman.

He kept coming until he felt the blaze of her body's heat all up and down his front, happier than he'd been since…man, he didn't even know when. Annette was drifting more firmly into his past, and the more he looked into Livia's beautiful face, the more appropriate it seemed that he turn the page on that first part of his life. It didn't mean that he hadn't loved Annette. It just meant that he had more living to do, with Livia.

"Is it safe in that big truck with you?"

"Absolutely not."

Another laugh. "Let's go then."

After he'd loaded the bike into the bed, he snapped his fingers as though he'd just remembered something. "I forgot to mention one little thing. Sorry."

"And what's that?"

"Payment. You don't think you can ride in my truck for free, do you?"

Her face fell into a pretty pout. "Oh, no. I'm not sure I have any money with me."

He shrugged. "I'll try to be flexible. What do you have to offer?"

"What did you have in mind?"

This time, he was the one to pull off his sunglasses. Taking his sweet time about it, he let his lazy gaze drift over her. To the drops of sweat gathered in the hollow between her collarbones; he wanted to lick those. To her beaded nipples under that little top; he wanted to lick those, too. To the *V* between her legs where he wanted to bury himself to the hilt. Now.

The hot pulse of his blood wouldn't leave him alone until he did.

"What do you think I have in mind?"

A wicked light flickered to life in her eyes. Her lips curled with the beginnings of a smile and that smile widened when she checked him out below the waist and saw how hard he was behind the tight button front of his jeans, how ready.

"Well," she said softly, "I always try to pay my debts."

"Glad to hear it."

Taking her hand, he pressed it to his erection, which was all the encouragement she needed. She stroked him up and down, rough, the way he needed it, and if that wasn't enough to drive him to the brink of insanity and several miles beyond, she jerked his head down with her free hand, opening her mouth so he could slide his tongue inside and taste her.

Lord. She was hot and slick, minty fresh and delicious. And suddenly playtime was over and he couldn't wait. Breaking the kiss, he towed her around to the rear door, which he opened.

"Have I introduced you to my backseat?"

She hesitated, taking inventory. Her gaze scanned the long stretch of deserted road in both directions, the protective overhang of tree branches and the truck's blacked-out windows. Then she eyed the spacious and comfy stretch of leather seat and, finally, the front of his jeans.

The decision apparently made, she looked him in the eye.

And peeled that stretchy top off over her head, baring her breasts to him. Dry-mouthed and astonished, he glanced to the cloudless blue sky overhead and said a silent thanks to whoever was responsible for Livia's appearance in his life. After that, he had a quick second to enjoy the way those plump handfuls bounced back into place and her nipples darkened and tightened down into jutting buds before she bent and, still watching him, shimmied out of her shorts and shoes, straightened, and stood before him in all her considerable glory. "Jesus," he muttered.

You'd think that after all their long nights together, the sight of this body might be losing its breathtaking effect on him, but no. You might also think that sex two or three times a day for a man who'd spent the last several years having sex once a month, if he was lucky, would be more than enough, but no. And if you thought having constant sex with Livia made him want to do anything other than have more sex with Livia, you were dead wrong.

Creeping closer, she went to work on freeing him from his pants. "Were we going to do this today, or…?"

"Hell, yeah."

He dove headfirst into the truck and pulled her in after him. Slamming the door shut, she straddled his lap and all but mauled him with her urgency. Her mouth caught his with aggressive, biting little kisses, and she rubbed her sweaty torso all over him, arching those breasts into his hands…his mouth…her own hands. Squeezing them together, she offered herself to him, brushing those hard nipples against his lips until, with a harsh groan, he sucked the way she liked.

"Ouch," she murmured. "Too hard. Take it easy on the girls, okay? You wore them out last night."

"How's this?" Trying to be gentler, he traced circles around her areola with his tongue. "That better?"

"Oh, yeah." Her head fell back—God, she was flexible—and she moaned and laughed in the most delicious combination his ears had ever heard.

Which was all well and good, but there was creamy white honey between her thighs—he could see it glisten and smell its musk—and he was dying here. Desperation making his movements choppy, he fished a condom out of his wallet and ripped it open with his teeth. He hated those little bastards, hated that there was a layer of anything between his flesh and hers, but he knew that wearing them was the right thing to do and—

"Wait," she said, slipping off his lap and to her knees on the floor in front of him. "Not so fast."

"Don't." Down to the last fumes of his control now, he couldn't possibly—

Too late.

Those dewy lips of hers slid down his length and sucked him inside, to the farthest, hottest part of her slick mouth, and he gasped with the unbearable pleasure. Damn near passed out.

"Livia," he croaked as his head fell back against the seat and his eyes rolled closed. "You have to stop." But the vibrating hum in her throat sounded suspiciously like smothered amusement and his hands were already twining into her damp hair to keep her bobbing head in place. "You have to…to…"

At that point he just shut the hell up. It was hard to launch a decent protest when you couldn't maintain blood flow to your brain. Limp and boneless except for his hands, which had curled into a death grip against her warm scalp, he accepted her gift until he absolutely couldn't take it another second.

"Come here."

She straddled his lap again and he rolled the condom on with lightning speed. The next thing he knew, he was buried to the base inside her, her frantically flexing ass was in his hands and her tongue was in his mouth.

At least for a few more thrusts, until the orgasm roared through her and she had to pull back and open her mouth to a high-pitched cry that was the world's best music. The sound of it, naturally, drove him over the edge, and he pumped and shouted until there was nothing left inside him except for his growing feelings for this woman.

Spent, they laid across the seat with her sprawled atop him like a rag doll.

After enough time had passed for them to catch their breath, she raised her head and gave him a kiss that was sweet and lingering.

"Hi," she said.

He grinned. "Hi."

"How was your day?"

As if she didn't know. "My day was excellent. Yours?"

"Oh, I'm having a great day. But I have a question for you."

"Oh, yeah?" This sounded like it could be serious, so he made a pillow by stacking his palms beneath his head. "What's that?"

"Are you ashamed of me?"

This was so unexpected that he couldn't stop a disbelieving snort. "What? No!"

"Have I embarrassed you?"

"*No.* Why would you ask—"

Sudden unhappiness darkened her eyes, turning the hazel muddy. "Because you haven't had me around your parents again and I'm getting the feeling you don't want me spending too much time with Kendra."

"Oh," he said, stunned and absolutely incapable of forming a decent answer. And then, because that wasn't lame enough, he said "Oh" again.

Silence, unless you counted her now red-hot cheeks, which all but sizzled with growing humiliation.

"Sorry," she backtracked, sitting up and grabbing her clothes. "I don't want to put you on the spot—"

"Livia."

His body protested the loss of her even as his floundering brain struggled for something acceptable to say. Options? Well, there was "I don't want you breaking my vulnerable daughter's heart when you go back to

L.A.," but that sounded too much like "I don't want you breaking my vulnerable heart when you go back to L.A.," and that, in turn, was too close to "Please don't ever leave me and go back to L.A.," and he wasn't ready to say that yet.

Hell, maybe he was only fooling himself. Maybe he'd been ready to say it since he'd laid eyes on her. But that didn't mean she was ready to scale back her career and the thrilling single life of fun and travel in favor of his cozy little ready-made family here in the country. And it also didn't mean that Kendra was ready for a new mommy.

How had they managed to duck and dodge the issue of the future of their relationship this whole time? And why couldn't he get a couple of words unstuck from his mouth before he completely blew it?

By the time he'd finished hemming and hawing, she had her clothes back on and her hurt face firmly in place. He may not have all the answers—yet—but he knew he'd sell his soul to the nearest passing demon to get her to smile again.

So he cupped her face and smoothed her silky cheek with his thumb.

"Hey," he said.

It took her a minute to flick her sulky gaze up to his. She raised a brow.

"Why don't you come for dinner at the big house with us tonight?"

"You don't want me."

"The hell I don't."

Thank God. For once he got something right; maybe it was the vehemence in his voice that did it. Whatever it was, she dimpled in the beginnings of a smile.

"We'll see," she told him. "I'll check my calendar and get back to you."

"Can you help me with my homework, Livia?" asked Kendra.

"*Miss* Livia," Hunter corrected.

Kendra, catching Livia's gaze, gave her an eye roll of utmost disgust. Livia, who was trying not to laugh and trying harder not to let Hunter see what she was doing, winked at the girl. Kendra laughed. And Hunter looked over from the kitchen counter, where he was pouring coffee with his mother, and frowned.

"What're you two females giggling about over there?"

"Nothing," answered Livia and Kendra together, doing a poor job of stifling more giggles. Hunter gave the two of them an exaggerated glare and then returned to what he'd been doing.

Livia couldn't stop grinning. The Chambers household was warm, loving and fun, and she'd enjoyed every minute of tonight's dinner there, even if she had put Hunter on the spot and basically forced him to invite her. What was a little lost pride when a night like this was at stake?

After welcoming her with smiles, hugs and mutterings about taking so long between visits, Mr. and Mrs. Chambers had treated her to flavorful beef stew, homemade biscuits and apple pie. Livia, feeling it was only polite, had eaten second helpings of everything, and was now stuffed like a Thanksgiving turkey. If there was a better way to spend a cool fall night, God hadn't invented it yet.

Now she sat in the leather chair closest to the great room fire, curled her legs under her and held her arms open for Kendra. The girl scrambled into her lap, bringing a hefty book with her, and settled in as though they'd spent a thousand other nights in this chair together. For extra coziness, Kendra pulled a fringed blanket off the back of the chair and spread it over their laps.

"There," she said, smoothing a last wrinkle and tucking one edge under Livia's thigh. "So you won't get cold."

"Thank you." Livia kissed the girl's cheek and took the book. "So what's the homework? I didn't even know first-graders had homework."

"I have to read for fifteen minutes." Kendra produced a small kitchen timer and set it. "You can listen."

"Okay. What're we reading? Oh, wait. Dumb question." She checked the book's spine and the tiny print. "*The Mammoth Book of Dinosaurs, Volume II.* Just a little light reading for a six-year-old, eh?"

The sarcasm went right over Kendra's head. "It's my favorite. I'm on page three-twelve."

"I hope you'll explain all the big words to me, girl," Livia said.

Livia flipped to the right page, glanced at Hunter

to see how he was coming along with her after-dinner coffee and got an unpleasant shock. On his way from the kitchen, with two steaming mugs in his hand, he'd paused to stare at a framed photograph that was at eye level on the bookshelf. The expression on his face was so rapt...so bleak...so lost...that she felt her heart contract in response.

Trying to pretend she didn't know what he was doing or that she'd never seen the picture didn't work. She'd seen it. It was a casual shot taken at his wedding to his dead wife, Annette. Wow. Even the other woman's name made her heart ache. *Annette,* Mrs. Chambers had told her. His wife's name was Annette. The name of Kendra's mother was Annette.

Annette.

It was one of those tight close-up shots of the two of them laughing into each other's faces, as though they couldn't believe their luck in finding each other and making it to such a fabulous day.

Annette, in her cloud of white, was the kind of beautiful and glowing bride that graced the pages of all those wedding magazines and catalogs. And the expression on Hunter's face in that frozen moment in time screamed things like love, passion and forever.

So there it was, in Livia's face for the first time: Hunter, the man she'd fallen in love with, had passionately loved and lost his wife, Annette. Now Annette was gone and Livia was here, and Hunter had never spoken his wife's name to her, not even once.

What did that mean? Nothing? Everything?

As though he felt the weight of her gaze on him, and the hurt, Hunter chose that moment to blink and snap himself out of it, giving Livia just enough time to look away and pretend she hadn't seen. If only it was that easy to erase the memory of his expression from her mind.

"Hey," he said, coming over and handing her the mug. "We didn't have that vanilla-flavored cream that you like, but—"

Whatever he may have said after that was lost to a wave of nausea that hit her the second that coffee smell hit her nose. It rose up out of nowhere, gagging on the back of her tongue, and for one horrified moment she saw herself spewing all that delicious food on Mrs. Chambers's polished floor.

Surging to her feet and unceremoniously dumping Kendra off her lap and into the chair, she hurried into the kitchen, poured herself a glass of water from the sink and took a couple of tentative sips.

"Livia?" Mr. Chambers, who'd been sweeping the floor, glanced around with concern. "You okay?"

"What's wrong, sweetie?" Mrs. Chambers hurried over and rubbed her shoulder.

Livia looked into their worried faces and called upon all her limited acting skills to force a cough and a smile. "I just, you know—" she coughed again and took another sip of water "—got strangled."

Relief brightened Hunter's face, but he kept a watchful eye on her, apparently ready to spring into some kind of action if another spell hit her. She stared into his face, wondering what the hell she'd do now because several things had just occurred to her and collectively added up to a huge issue.

One, she hadn't had a period in about six weeks.

Two, her breasts were unusually tender.

Three, the smell of coffee had just about made her vomit, and Mama always said that one of the earliest symptoms of pregnancy was an aversion to certain food smells.

Oh, God, she thought, stunned. *Oh, God*.

"Thanks for bringing me," Livia said. "I'll just be a minute."

"Take your time."

Hunter watched her disappear down the aisle into the depths of the pharmacy area and tried to use the time alone to collect his scattered thoughts. At some point between apple pie and this impromptu emergency trip to the twenty-four-hour drugstore for Livia to get several toiletries that she absolutely, positively had to have tonight, things had gone seriously wrong. A night that had begun so promisingly now seemed…bewildering.

Well, why pretend? He knew when things got weird. It was when he caught that unexpected glimpse of his wedding picture and Annette's image came back into sharp and painful focus for the first time in a while. For the first time since he'd begun falling for Livia.

Annette had been young and exuberant, the radiant sun at the center of his universe, and on that wonderful day so long ago, when he'd promised her forever, he'd had no idea that her forever would end in a few short years, snuffed out in a smashed car on a dark road.

Now here he was, still alive, and alive in a way he'd never been before, thanks to Livia. Was that okay? Was that fair? Was this the course his life was supposed to take?

Guilt and loss were part of his issue tonight.

The other part was primitive, gut-wrenching fear. It wasn't cool, a big guy like him being scared shitless, but it was real. Spending time with Livia and his family, seeing again how effortlessly she made herself at home and won the hearts of everyone around her, watching his daughter sit on her lap and snuggle with her…it was too freaking perfect. Too much of a dream come true to be real.

What if—and this was where the fear came in—what if it wasn't real? Livia's idyll here in the country with him was ending soon, and they'd managed to spend her time here making love and talking about everything in the world *except* where, if anywhere, this relationship was going. What if she thought it wasn't going anywhere? He'd barely managed to scrape his ruined heart up off the floor after Annette died. He didn't think he could do it again if Livia said goodbye and sailed back off to L.A., into the world where she belonged and he never would.

The killer was that this whole time he hadn't worked up the nerve to just ask her. How crazy was that? If you wanted to know what someone's plans were, and you had a question, the normal and sane thing to do was just ask. Except there was that fear again, keeping his throat on lockdown—because what the hell would he do if she blinked up at him with those gorgeous eyes and tried to let him down gently as she told him that she'd had fun in the country, thanks, but it was time for her to get back to the glitz and glamour of her real life?

Jesus.

His head felt like it was seconds away from explosion. Rubbing his hands over his temples didn't help and neither did pinching the bridge of his nose until he could all but feel the cartilage snap. Headache. He had the mother of all headaches.

And what was the solution to that overwhelming and complex problem, genius? How about you look around, since you're in the middle of a, you know, drugstore, and find some drugs? Didn't they always keep those little travel packets of aspirin and whatnot next to the candy in the checkout line? Why not look?

Abandoning his post holding up the customer service desk—what was taking Livia so long? Had she been abducted out the back door?—he went to the nearest open checkout lane and skimmed the offerings. Candy… candy…more candy…lighters…dangling air fresheners for the car…tabloids…tissue packets…

Wait.

Go back.

With dread inching up his spine and creeping across his scalp, he shifted his gaze back to the tabloids. He knew they were trash, yeah, and that he was having a vulnerable moment here and that he shouldn't look closer. If he was smart and had a single self-protective molecule in his body, he'd just walk away and pretend he'd seen nothing.

Only he'd never been one for being an ostrich.

Shooting a quick glance around to make sure Livia wasn't returning right this very second, he grabbed the ridiculous magazine with hands that were suddenly both damp and shaky and looked down into the smiling face of the woman who, it turned out, he only partially knew. And got a nice kick-in-the-gut glimpse into the other part of her life.

There she was, at a table at one of those glittering parties, looking like a million sexy bucks, with the hair, the makeup and the skimpy little dress that tastefully hinted at one of the world's greatest bodies. There was the obligatory champagne glass and there was the inevitable NBA MVP grinning and whispering something in her ear as she laughed.

To tie the image up into a nice fat bow for him, there was the caption, which was just enough to knock the remaining wind out of his sails: "Athletes and Their Supermodels—Why These Relationships Work."

Chapter 13

Pregnant. She was pregnant.

Livia stared at the plus sign on the little pee stick thingee, trapped in a weird world between fierce joy and abject terror. She was going to be a mother. Hysterical laughter bubbled up in her throat, but since Hunter was on the other side of that bathroom door and she didn't want to babble like a loon, she clapped her hand over her mouth and choked it back.

A baby. There was a baby inside her. She'd made a baby with the man she loved.

Did she look different? Staring hard at her reflection in the mirror, she didn't think so. Well, except for that glowing happiness on her face. That was different, but, in fairness, Hunter had put that there long before she'd known there was a baby.

How had this happened? They'd used condoms, all except that first time on the dock, but, as they'd taught her in health class in fifth grade, one time was all it took. What about the pill, though? She religiously took it every morning, right after she brushed her teeth and she never missed a day. Ever. So how on earth did—

Oh, wait. Oh, God. It was the antibiotics she'd taken to get rid of that never-ending sinus infection from hell that did it. Hadn't the doctor mentioned that she'd need to use other forms of birth control when he'd written the prescription all those weeks ago? Since she'd been celibate with no prospects at the time, the advice had gone in one ear and out the other. Too bad the doctor hadn't had a crystal ball in his office. Then he could have warned her that she'd soon be having nonstop wild sex and needed to be more careful.

So what did she do—

"Livia?" Hunter called from the living room. "Did you fall in or what?"

Peeking her head around the door, she tried to sound normal. "Sorry! I'll be out in a second."

"Hurry up," he grumbled. "It's lonely out here."

"Okay."

Okay. She shut the door again and tried to think. What did she do? Should she tell him now or should she confirm with her doctor before she went off half-cocked? Maybe she wasn't pregnant after all, and this would be a big scare for nothing.

The blaring red *99% accurate!* on the blue box in the trash can put an end to that desperate speculation.

Yeah, she was pregnant. In addition to the breast thing and the nausea thing, she just knew. There was a baby in there. And she couldn't be happier about it.

Still, they'd never talked about their future and she was supposed to leave for Mexico soon. Hunter couldn't very well run the winery from L.A., but he hadn't asked her to stay here with him, either.

Other *hadn'ts?*

He hadn't told her he loved her.

He hadn't raised the subject of their future.

He hadn't exposed her to his daughter and his parents except in very small doses, as though he didn't want them getting the wrong idea about her place in his life.

He hadn't ever talked about Annette and whether he was over her.

He hadn't looked like he was over Annette when he'd stared at their wedding picture earlier.

The doubts crept, one by one, into her mind, banding together and gathering strength to use against her, like a pitchfork-carrying mob. When they'd all assembled, they formed one unmistakable truth:

Hunter might not be happy about this.

What the hell would she do then?

The distant bleat of her cell phone distracted her, pulling her away from her increasingly dark thoughts. She should get that. It might be Rachel calling about tomorrow's arrival time, assuming, of course, that it wasn't Rachel calling to say, yet again, that she wasn't coming.

Taking a deep breath, she hurried out to the living room, where Hunter was sprawled on the sofa watching ESPN and looking sulky, with Willard drowsing on the floor at his feet. They both looked around at her appearance and Hunter picked her blinking cell phone up from the coffee table and passed it to her.

"Thanks." She glanced at the display. "It's my agent. I'll just be a minute, okay?"

His jaw tightened. There was definitely something off about him tonight; was it the whole wedding picture thing still? Maybe. She'd have to ask after she got off the phone.

"Okay," he said, his gaze shifting back to the TV.

Clicking the phone on, she headed back into the bedroom. "Hey, Susan."

"How's Napa?" Susan asked in her usual crisp tone. She'd never been one for niceties and always wanted to get them out of the way ASAP so she could get to the only part of any conversation that interested her: money. "You ready to get back to work?"

"Well," Livia began.

"We need you in Cabo in two days for the fittings, right? So you'd better start packing your little bags. Or were you going home first?"

God. Livia slumped on the bed and rested her head in her hands, sudden exhaustion making her crazy. Ten minutes ago she'd discovered she was pregnant with a man who'd never even said he loved her and she was supposed to talk travel logistics and photo shoots?

"I'll just go straight there."

"Good. And Giancarlo's hosting a dinner party for you that night. Only about fifty people, nothing big."

"A party?" Was this some sort of a cruel joke? Another stupid dinner party given by another one of her idle-rich friends when her life was at such a dramatic crossroads? "This is the first I'm hearing about that."

"It's an early surprise. For your birthday. So don't let on, okay?"

"Fine."

"I'll call you tomorrow to check in."

Checking in was Susan-speak for accepting a ridiculous number of new assignments and scheduling Livia's time for the next six months or so. Since Livia would be preparing to give birth, and since she'd already decided to take an extended break from modeling even before she found out she was pregnant, she'd have to put the kibosh on that plan, but it could wait until tomorrow. One big conversation per night was all she could handle, and she and Hunter had a baby that needed discussing.

"Great," she told Susan. "Bye."

Hanging up, she went back to the living room and perched on the coffee table in front of Hunter. He sat up, looking grim, turned off the TV and swung his feet to the floor. Willard yawned his overwhelming enthusiasm for her arrival and went back to sleep.

"Hi," she said. "Maybe we should talk."

"You're leaving," he said flatly.

"Yeah. I have a photo shoot in Cabo San Lucas. It's been scheduled for a while."

"And a party."

So he'd heard that, eh? "There's always a party."

"I see."

Those golden eyes of his were dark now, and his shoulders were so rigid that they might have been replaced with a slab of concrete. The tension radiating from him felt black and dangerous, like a negative force field, and she watched him scrub his hands over his head and across his tight jaw with growing anxiety.

Finally he met her gaze and they stared at each other for several beats. The whole time she searched for a sign of the laughing man who'd made love to her in his truck earlier that day, tried to find evidence of his existence, but he was so far gone right now he might have only ever been a figment of her imagination. Right now, the only thing she could see was the cold, aloof man who'd confronted her in the parking lot the day they met, and it terrified her.

"What's wrong?" she whispered.

He shrugged and raised a wry eyebrow, and the gestures were so casual and unspeakably wrong for this moment that they were like slaps to the face.

"So this is it, then."

She licked her dry lips and took a deep breath, trying to formulate a scenario where those words and that detached look on his face didn't add up to things being over between them.

"This is...*it?*" she echoed.

"Well, we knew it couldn't last, right? Now it's time

for you to leave Napa and go back to your shoots and your parties and your life."

"What about you?"

Another dismissive shrug. "I'll stay here."

Oh, God. Blinking back sudden hot tears, she looked at Willard's sleeping body and tried to pull it together. Falling apart now wouldn't solve anything and neither would begging. Though her pride told her to keep her big mouth shut and not make this moment more awkward than it needed to be, her stupid heart forced her to reach out, to try.

"But we'll see each other, right? We can fly back and forth because it's only a couple of hours, and I don't see why we couldn't—"

A crooked smile distorted one corner of his mouth. "What's the point?"

"I thought the point was that we cared about each other. Am I wrong?"

That, for the first time, put a dent in his composure. Resting his elbows on his knees, he dropped his head between his hands and squeezed his temples so hard she was surprised she didn't hear his skull crack.

Forever passed, and then another forever, and then he raised his now red face and ran his tongue along his lower lip in a clear attempt to keep his composure. It didn't work. He was fighting back a grimace that made him look like there was something disgusting in his mouth that he needed to spit out.

"This isn't about us caring for each other." He wouldn't look at her and could barely get the words out, his voice was so rough with gravel. "This is about what will work and what won't work."

Okay. Okay, so she needed a minute to choke back the rising sob of frustration and fear, and for some of the burning in her throat to cool enough for her to talk. *Breathe, girl. Breathe. You can do this. Think of the baby.*

Blinking furiously and pressing her lips together until they'd gone numb, which was better than the quivering they'd been doing, she focused on the logical argument. "If we care for each other enough, Hunter, we can make it work."

At last he looked at her and she wished he hadn't. His golden eyes were nothing but a sheet of ice now, a wall of amber behind which he'd locked himself down so tight she'd never be able to get close to him.

"How can it work?" His tone was so light and conversational they could have been discussing whether a three-pronged plug could fit into a two-pronged outlet. "You think I'd ask you to sacrifice your career for me? Or maybe you think I'd be just fine leaving the winery and, I don't know, spending my days on the beach in Malibu and my nights attending movie premieres and restaurant openings with you? Is that it?"

Wow.

Way to hit below the belt, Hunter. Way to slice through all her attempts at compromise and make her feel vulnerable, foolish and, best of all, shallow. If ever there was a time for her to just shut up and walk away, this was it, but she just couldn't let him go. What they had together couldn't be destroyed so easily.

So she swiped away the embarrassing tears that trickled down her cheeks, took yet another deep breath and swallowed enough of her remaining pride to try again.

"It doesn't have to be about sacrifice. This is my last shoot for a while and then my calendar is free. I could do whatever I wanted. And they have these newfangled inventions called airplanes, don't they? We both have cell phones and e-mail. Why couldn't we try for a while and see how—"

He stared at her with not one spark of pity in his hard eyes. "When did a long-distance relationship ever work?" he wondered. "And how could my young daughter and I fit into your glamorous world of celebrities and fashion and parties?"

Something snapped inside her. Broke neatly down the middle, leaving the two ruined parts to disintegrate to dust. Much as she'd wanted to be calm, gracious and classy, she couldn't do it when he was this anxious to destroy everything they'd shared.

"Those are just *excuses,*" she shrieked. "Excuses! If you don't love me enough to try, then why don't you just say—"

"Don't." The big L-word made his mouth contort with disbelief or discomfort or something terrible like that, but, hey, at least he didn't laugh right in her face. "Don't do this, Livia."

A lightbulb went off over her head, bringing this

whole situation into terrible HDTV clarity, and she had to ask, even if the truth killed her.

"This is about Annette, isn't it?"

The name made him flinch and wasn't that a clue enough for her dimwitted brain? "What about Annette?"

"I saw you." The rising hysteria was making her voice shake and she backed off for a minute, shuddering with her effort to remain rational and lower the volume. "I saw the way you looked at her picture tonight."

Cursing, he dropped his head again, squeezing it between his fisted hands as though he'd love nothing better than to smash his skull and end this excruciating conversation. Which was just too damn bad because he owed her at least this much of an explanation.

"And I'm wondering if you're not over her yet. I'm wondering if you'll ever be over her."

When he raised his head this time, he was deathly pale and still, his eyes feverishly bright. And his voice was absolute and unyielding as he threw a live grenade into the middle of all her hopes and dreams, blowing them to kingdom come.

"No," he said softly. "I'll never get over my wife."

Livia consulted her list in the bright morning sunlight and surveyed her bag, which was packed to the gills with various little Napa Valley purchases and would, therefore, be a lot harder to close and zip than it'd been when she came nearly a month ago. Her toiletries were still in the bathroom, but she'd remembered her camera, her shoes, not that she'd brought that many pairs, and her Jackie Robinson biography, so she could cross all those off the list. The only other things were—

Someone knocked at the front door.

Since it wasn't Hunter's brisk and assertive knock, she didn't really care who it was, but the car to take her to the airport may have come a little early so she should probably answer it.

Taking a final inventory as she passed through the living room—no forgotten shoes half-hidden under the sofa, thank goodness—she opened the door.

"Rachel!"

Screeching like ten-year-olds, they latched on and hugged as though they hadn't seen each other for fifty years of desperate searching. Since Livia was a giantess and Rachel was a cute little pixie, Livia swept her off her feet and swung her in a circle, which Rachel tolerated with good grace. Then Livia plunked her back down and, keeping her at arm's length, checked her out to see how she was doing.

Boy, was she glad to see her.

She needed a friend after the horrible night she'd had.

"You look great." Livia smoothed Rachel's dark Halle Berry hair and admired her turquoise necklace; Rachel always wore the prettiest artsy jewelry and whatnot, which probably had something to do with her eye for color and her success as a makeup artist. If you wanted a great accessory, Rachel was the one to consult. "I thought you weren't coming until later."

"We got bumped up to an earlier flight."

"Come on in." Taking her hand, Livia led Rachel into the living room, where they both sat on the sofa. "What's new? What'd you decide about the wedding? You got my e-mailed pictures of the chapel and all, right?"

"Yup. It'll be here in about a month."

"A month!"

"Oh, and the merger is going through."

Wow. So Limelight Entertainment Management, the agency that represented Livia and had been started by Rachel's parents before their death twenty-five years ago, would merge with their rivals at A.F.I.

Sophia, Rachel's sister and second-in-command at Limelight Entertainment Management, *hated* A.F.I. and had been fighting her uncle for months, arguing against the merger.

This was going to be interesting.

"I can't believe it," Livia said. "I never thought it'd happen."

"Tell me about it."

"Where's Ethan?"

"He's catching up with Hunter."

"Oh, yeah?" Livia glued that painful smile on her face and focused on keeping her expression from falling at the mere mention of his name. If she didn't watch it, she'd slip up and do something to clue Rachel in that she'd just had the love affair of her life, and she wasn't ready to discuss Hunter, her feelings for him or the baby with anyone. Not even Rachel. "Did you meet him?"

"Yeah. It's a shame he's so ugly. A real tragedy."

Livia tried to laugh.

"But is he always this glum? He looked like he'd lost his best friend, his house and his dog. Is that what running a winery does to a person?"

Livia shrugged, her gaze shifting away from Rachel's. This was dangerous territory and they really needed to talk about something else.

"Come to think of it," Rachel said, taking a closer look at Livia's face with those eagle eyes of hers, "he looked a lot like you look. Have you been crying? You have, haven't you? Your eyes are all swollen."

"Rachel," Livia began, trying to work up a plausible denial but it was already too late.

"Oh, my God! You and Hunter?" Rachel clapped her hands over her mouth, trying to stifle a giggle of startled comprehension and excitement. "I'm right! There's something going on with you, isn't there?"

"I can't get into it, Rachel."

"But—"

"Rachel." Livia held up a hand, pressed her lips together and struggled not to cry. "Please. I can't do this right now. Please understand."

"Oh, honey." Rachel squeezed her arm in a show of concerned support. "Do I need to kill him for you?"

Livia spluttered out a laugh. "I'll let you know, okay? Right now, I just need to get out of here. I think Mexico will do me some good."

Sometime during the long and difficult night, when she wasn't replaying the coldness in Hunter's eyes and the lack of inflection in his voice as he hit her with the joyous news that he'd never be over his dead wife, she'd convinced herself that the trip to Mexico, though inconvenient, was exactly what she needed.

She'd throw herself into her work, get some sun and think. The time away would give her some perspective and, hopefully, enough emotional distance to manage this situation. In a few days, she'd come back, tell Hunter she was pregnant and would raise the baby whether he decided to be involved in their lives or not, and it would all be good.

In a few days.

Right now, though, all was not good.

"How about another hug?" she asked Rachel. "I could use one."

"You got it, girl."

Holding her arms wide, Rachel pulled her in close, and Livia, feeling exhausted and empty, rested her head against the reassuring warmth of her friend's chest and wished she could stay there forever.

Chapter 14

This was so hard.

This was so incredibly, unspeakably, unbelievably hard.

Livia loitered outside the doghouse, blinking back her tears and trying not to fall apart. Kendra had ignored her with steadfast determination for the last five minutes and Livia was nearing the end of her depleted emotional reserves.

"Kendra," she called again. "Please."

No answer from the dark depths of the doghouse. The flashlight was out today, intensifying the gloom inside. Even Willard, who was also in there with Kendra, had his face turned away from Livia, as though she was also letting him down and he didn't plan to let her forget it anytime soon, if ever.

Swiping at her face, she made a quick decision and sat down. "If I'm not welcome in the dragon's den today," she said, "I'll just sit by the entrance. I hope that's okay."

No answer but at least now she could see what was going on in the den. Kendra sat in the far corner, with Willard's big head in her lap and her stuffed diplodocus hugged to her chest above that. As Livia peered inside, Kendra stared off in the other direction, resolutely refusing to either acknowledge her presence or accept her goodbye.

It hurt. In a twenty-four-hour period that had pretty much maxed her out on the hurt thing, what with that final talk with Hunter, the all-night crying and a poignant goodbye to Mr. and Mrs. Chambers, the wounded silence from Kendra was, quite possibly, the worst. Was this what she'd been like when her mother died? Was this what Hunter had had to overcome? How had he managed it?

"Kendra." Swiping away another of her never-ending tears, she focused on not sniffling and keeping her voice upbeat. "I have to go to Mexico for my work, okay? I really wish I could stay here and play with you for a little while longer but I have to do my job. Can you understand that? It's like when you have to go to school. Sometimes you don't want to go, but you have to anyway. And I don't want to leave here, but I have to anyway."

Kendra pressed her lips into the green fur of her stuffed animal and said nothing.

"But I'm going to send you a postcard when I get

there. And they have lots of fossils and stuff in Mexico, so I'll see if I can find one for you. And maybe a dinosaur T-shirt. Could that work, do you think?"

Kendra shrugged.

Oh, thank God! A shrug was communication, right? It wasn't a sentence or anything but it was a definite step up from being ignored, wasn't it?

"Kendra," she said helplessly. "You're a wonderful girl. I'm going to miss you so much." *I love you. I wish you were mine. I wish your father wanted me enough to let me into your life a little more.* "Can I please give you a hug before I go?"

This time the communication was a lot more painful: Kendra scooted farther into the corner, away from Livia. The sight of that tiny little figure so stiff with disapproval and disappointment was more than Livia could take. Dropping her head into her hands, she gave in to the despair and sobbed as quietly as she could manage, grateful that Kendra wasn't looking and hopefully didn't know that she'd fallen apart.

But three seconds of that nonsense was enough. She needed to work on getting her emotions under control. No time like the present, right? Wiping her face dry, she tried to smile and tried harder to keep her voice upbeat and positive.

"Bye for now, Kendra."

If only she could tell the girl that she'd be back soon when she returned to tell Hunter about the baby. If only she could tell her that she'd become a big sister next year. If only Hunter would share his wonderful family with her and maybe let Kendra visit her in L.A. when the baby came. If only…

Wow. She had enough *if onlys* to fill up a stadium, didn't she?

"Bye, Willard." The dog, at least, looked around to acknowledge her existence. When she held her hand out to him, he crawled forward on his belly and let her scratch his soft ears one last time. From here on out, she'd have to watch *The Dog Wrangler* by herself and that would never be as much fun as enjoying it with him. "Silly dog."

Okay, Livia. Stop stalling. Time to go.

She stood, dusted off her jeans and headed for the cottage to grab her bag. She'd turned in her rental bike already and printed her boarding pass. The only thing—

Running footsteps came up behind her and she turned and saw Kendra sprinting after her. With an incoherent cry of happiness, she stooped in time to catch her and swung her up into her arms, thrilled with the weight and heat of that sturdy little body and the sweetness of her skin and the fruity fragrance of her twisted hair.

"I love you, Kendra." Livia kissed those fat little cheeks over and over again and let the words come, because they were the truth and the girl had the right to know. "I love you."

Kendra wrapped her strong arms around Livia's neck, nearly strangling her with affection, and she hung on for much longer than Livia ever could have hoped.

Then she pulled back and offered Livia her stuffed diplodocus.

"Take him with you," she said. "He's always wanted to see Mexico."

"Can someone tell me who died?"

Hunter, who was sitting at his parents' kitchen table at the B and B, looked up from the cup of stone-cold cappuccino he'd been nursing for the last half hour and glared at his younger brother. With his usual flair for the dramatic, Ethan was standing in the middle of the room, putting on a show. Though Hunter was glad to see him, he'd have to cut the youngster down to size if he kept up like this.

"I mean," Ethan continued, "what could be wrong? The grapes are harvested, the prodigal son—that would be me—is back and the sun is shining. Where are the smiles and the laughter? What the hell's gotten into you people?"

"Watch your language," muttered Mom, who was manning the cappuccino machine. "I don't know what they teach you in L.A., but around here, we don't swear."

"Damn right." Dad, who was pouring a bowl of kibble for Willard, winked.

"We'll get right to work on killing that fatted calf for you, Ethan," Hunter said. "Would that make you feel better? What about a parade?"

"A parade would work." Ethan accepted a steaming

cup from Mom, leaned against the counter and sipped appreciatively. "I'm serious, though. What's wrong?"

Mom put her hands on her hips and frowned over at Hunter. "Should you tell him or should I?"

Ah, shit. Mom had been in a rare mood ever since Livia stopped by to say goodbye earlier, and the last thing he needed right now was Mom launching into him in front of everyone. No good could come of that. He already felt like he was crawling out of his skin what with Livia leaving to resume her glamorous life far away from him.

Even now he couldn't quite believe it.

Livia was gone. She'd gotten on a plane and flown away. Just like that. And had he begged her to stay? Had he told her he loved her? Had he thrown his body in front of the plane to stop it from taxiing down the runway?

Hell, no.

He'd done everything but plant his foot in her ass as she walked out the door, and now he couldn't shake the sickening feeling that he'd made the worst mistake of his life. At the time, he'd thought that a clean break was best. Now he felt like he'd cut off his right hand for no good reason.

Still, he didn't plan to spill his guts to this crowd.

"There's nothing to—" Hunter began.

Mom snorted with disgust and waved him to silence. "Hunter found a wonderful girl," she explained to Ethan. "We all loved her. Livia Blake—"

Ethan goggled. "What? *Livia?*"

"Sweetest girl in the world. Now they've had a falling

out and Livia left. God knows if we'll ever see her again. And this one—" Mom jerked her thumb in Hunter's general direction, apparently too irritated by his actions to look at him directly "—just let her go." She snapped her fingers. "Just like that. *Idiot.*"

Great. Now, on top of Livia leaving, Kendra falling into the depths of despair and his own broken heart to nurse, his own mother thought he was an idiot. It was shaping up to be quite a day, wasn't it?

Ethan clunked his mug on the counter and looked at Hunter with alarm. "Is that true?"

Dad, now patting Willard's hindquarters while the dog crunched loudly over his bowl, answered for him. "It's true," he said grimly.

Okay. That was enough.

"First of all," Hunter said, raising a hand to stop this discussion before it got any further out of hand, "I can speak for myself. Second, my personal life isn't up for discussion, so let's just drop this—"

"Yeah, but who knew you had a personal life since Annette died?" Ethan interjected. "I think that's worth discussing. Livia, eh?" He tipped his head, giving the matter serious consideration. "She's great. I actually think she'd be a good match for you. What happened?"

"Did you just hear me say that I'm not discussing—"

"I don't know," Mom answered, ignoring his statement. "Getting this one—" another thumb jerk in

Hunter's direction "—to talk is like getting blood from a stone."

The three of them gave him baleful stares. Hell, even the dog paused in his chomping to nail him with a look that said, quite plainly, *You dumbass,* and the negative attention was more than he could take. He was sick to death here because Livia was gone and he'd sent her away, but even if he got her back, he didn't see how it could work.

He exploded. "Do I look happy? Why the hell are you blaming me? If any of you geniuses know how I can run a winery while Livia is flying all over the world, going to her little parties and whatnot, then I'd love to hear."

Both Mom and Ethan stared at him as though he'd begun babbling in pig Latin.

"That girl doesn't want to fly around and go to parties," Mom said, aghast.

"Yeah," Ethan agreed. "She's not a partier anymore. I'd have heard—L.A.'s a small town. And Rachel claims she's phasing out the modeling. I'm not sure about that."

"That girl helped me with the dishes." Mom ticked off her points on her fingers. "She asked for my beef stew recipe. She wanted to talk about how Kendra's doing in school and she grilled me about what I do here at the winery. It's as plain as the nose on my face that she's got her mind on family and children. How much partying can a person do, anyway? I'm betting she's got all that out of her system and now she's ready to settle down. Too bad you let her go."

Stunned and deeply disturbed, Hunter planted his elbows on the table and rested his head in his hands. Could any of that be true? More unbearable was the possibility that it was all true and he was such an idiot that he'd never even discussed it with Livia.

Mom was right about the sorry state of his mental prowess, wasn't she? He was such a genius he'd never even asked Livia what she wanted or if she'd consider staying here with him. He'd been so afraid of her rejection that he'd preempted it with a rejection of his own.

And then when he saw that tabloid photo last night…

"I have a daughter to consider," he reminded everyone.

"Kendra and Livia love each other, boy," Dad said. "Can't you see that?"

Yeah, he'd seen it. Maybe he hadn't known what to make of it but he'd definitely seen it.

The question was: What should he do now? He rubbed the top of his head, wishing he could make his brain work and kick out some sort of a plan, a solution, but he just couldn't.

"Oh, I get it," Ethan said in that soft taunt that only brothers could manage. "He's scared."

This accusation was, naturally, a red cape to a bull, and Hunter snapped his head up, ready to throw down in front of God, Mom and everybody.

"I am *not*—"

To his surprise, Ethan smiled, and it wasn't a sneering

smirk or anything like it. It was the understanding expression of a man who'd been there himself and knew what it felt like to walk in those shoes. "Let me tell you something, my brother. I didn't want to fall in love. Trust me. I wanted to try all the women I could get my hands on—"

"I'm not hearing this," Mom said loudly.

"But life's short, you know? And if you're lucky enough to find the right woman—actually, you're lucky enough to find *another* right woman, aren't you? You gonna throw that away? You think that's what Annette would want? You don't think she'd be glad to know that a great woman was taking care of her little girl?"

Shit. That actually made sense. A whole lot of freaking sense. Why hadn't he seen it that way last night? What was wrong with him?

Mom gave him a pitying look. She could probably detect that his overwhelmed circuits were about to melt down and wanted to give him a reprieve to gather his thoughts.

"Let's give the boy a minute," she told the others. "He needs to—"

Purposeful rubberized footsteps came into the kitchen just then, and they all glanced around in time to see Kendra arrive, looking grim and determined.

Oh, Lord. What now?

She wore her little pink Windbreaker and carried that same square suitcase from the other week. Willard's leash was in her other hand and she wasted no time clipping it onto the dog's collar.

"Ah, Kendra?" Hunter asked, not at all sure he wanted to know. "What're you doing?"

"I'm running away. Can you take me and Willard to the airport right now?"

Inside his chest, his heart began to pound. With fear, yeah, and with trepidation because he'd dug himself a pretty big hole with Livia last night, but mostly with hope. "Why, sweetie?"

"We want to go to Mexico and bring Livia back," Kendra informed him.

"Why?" he asked again.

"Because Willard and I want her to be our new mommy."

Chapter 15

There she was. Finally. Thank goodness.

Relief overwhelmed Hunter, roaring through him like an avalanche down a mountainside. He was lucky it didn't knock him flat on his butt.

After prying Livia's itinerary and trip details out of Rachel—who didn't seem too keen on him, to tell the truth—he'd scrounged up his passport, thrown a few clothes in his overnight bag and caught the next available flight south, which wasn't until late that night. There'd been no delays, praise be to God, because in his current state of high agitation and extreme nervousness, he'd probably have flipped out and run afoul of the flight attendants if the captain had reported mechanical trouble or cloudy skies.

He'd landed, taken a cab to the swanky hotel where

Livia was staying and decided to wait, just a little while longer, and take the time to decompress and gather his thoughts so he didn't blow it again—which, given his unfortunate record when it came to communicating with Livia, was a distinct possibility.

Now here he was, on a white beach in front of a startling backdrop of sparkling aquamarine water beneath a sky of piercing blue, and there she was, doing her job, not fifty feet away.

He wasn't the only avid onlooker, which shouldn't have surprised him but did. Standing on the periphery in a crowd of about fifty people, he watched the photo shoot, which was quite the production. A photographer and a videographer both stood barefoot in the lapping surf, getting their shots and murmuring words of encouragement. Miscellaneous other people surrounded them—probably makeup people and stylists and the like.

In the center of it all, like a statue of a goddess on a dais, was Livia.

Her hair was wild and blowing free, and her skin had already acquired a tropical glow that it hadn't had in Napa. Draped over an outcropping of black rock, posing for the camera with utmost concentration—smiling… pouting…seducing—she wore a red bikini that he'd be wet-dreaming about for the rest of his life.

She was a glittering jewel. A siren. A dream.

But then the clouds shifted, the photographer said, "That's it. We've lost the light," and she took off her supermodel's mask as though she'd unzipped her dress, stepped out of it and hung it in the closet.

The sultry expression left her face and she was, suddenly, just Livia, the woman he loved. But the light was gone from her eyes and her shoulders drooped. She was lost and forlorn but struggling to do her best, and he was to blame.

He'd made her sad but, with God's help, he'd spend the rest of his life making her happy.

Hit with a sudden inspiration, he blended into the crowd surging forward for her autograph and waited for his chance.

"Livia! This way, Livia! Sign this!"

One of the stylists passed her a tie-dyed sarong and Livia made a dress out of it, wrapping it underneath her arms and tying it in the front. Then she plastered that damn smile—each fake smile these days felt like it was taking twenty years off her life, no joke—back on her face, waved at the people who'd come to watch the shoot and wandered over to sign a few autographs and pose for a few quick camera-phone shots. Exhaustion and growing nausea (this baby was really starting to make himself known, the little stinker) were no reasons to ignore her fans and act like a diva.

"Hi, guys," she said, accepting markers and scrawling her name on whatever surface was thrust her way, which included T-shirts, iPods, scraps of paper and, notably, the bare shoulder blade of a scrawny teenage American boy who swore he'd never shower again. "Are you enjoying Mexico? Yeah? *Que pasa?*"

It went on. And on.

"Sign this, Livia."

Another hand thrust forward, passing her a folded cocktail napkin from the hotel. Raising her pen, she started to sign it, but there was already huge block writing on it: "Marry me."

Ah, geez. Another marriage proposal from a starstruck, hormone-poisoned fan. What photo shoot would be complete without at least one man begging her to marry him? At least he hadn't asked for her bikini bottoms or anything. She looked up, ready to let the guy down easily and call for one of the bodyguards if necessary—

"Oh, God," she cried, clapping her hand over her mouth to choke back the sob before it erupted.

It was Hunter.

Hunter.

With a cry, she threw herself into the crowd and at him, possibly knocking several people to the sand in her enthusiasm; she didn't know and didn't care. Then his arms were closing around her, holding her too tight, hurting her, and she could only laugh and cry as he rained kisses all over her face, all but choking on her emotion.

"You came, Hunter. I can't believe it. You're here."

"Where can we talk?" he whispered urgently in her ear.

"Over here."

Taking his hand and ignoring the disgruntled murmurs of the last couple of fans, she towed him to the other side of a folding screen beneath a huge palm frond umbrella. This was where she'd changed and it wasn't exactly a private room, but it would do for now. The second the crowd was out of view, he grabbed her face in his hands and kissed her, which was no easy job since they were both crying.

"I'm sorry." Pulling back at last, he swiped at his eyes and tried to get control. "I've got some begging to do."

"You sure do," she said, doing her best to look furious through her face-splitting smile. "What have you got to say for yourself?"

"I should be on my knees after what I said the other night."

"Well, why don't you correct the record right now?"

"I'm happy to. I love you. You know that, right?"

"Oh, God," she said, sobbing again.

"After the accident, I really thought my life was over. I wanted it to be over—"

"Don't say that."

"I didn't think I'd ever be happy again, and I certainly never thought I'd find a woman who makes my heart stop in a way no one else has ever done before."

"But why?" Holding his hard cheeks between her hands, she stared up into his turbulent eyes and tried to understand what he'd said and done. "Why did you act like you'd never be over Annette?"

"Because I was scared," he said simply, the confession stunning her. "Why would a woman like you want to be with a man like me when you've got this—" he flapped a hand toward the shoot and the fans "—this life?"

Silly man. "Why? Because I'm crazy in love with you, and your daughter, and your winery and your parents. Oh, and your dog. That's why."

"So…maybe you'd want to live there with us?"

"That'd be nice. Since that was my last shoot and I won't have much income anymore. It'd be great to have somewhere to stay."

"I'm not asking you to give up—"

"I'd already decided before I ever went to Napa. The modeling thing is over. Been there, done that. Yawn."

"Are you sure?"

"Oh, I'm sure." She hesitated but now was as good a time to tell him as ever. "Besides. Kendra and the new baby deserve a full-time mother, don't you think?"

"Speaking of Kendra, that girl tried to get me to take her and the dog to the airport so she could fly down here and—wait, *what? What* did you say?"

Taking his hand, she pressed it to her stomach. "I'm saying that Chambers Winery is a fertile place. Must be something in the air. I hope that's okay with you."

"Okay?" His voice cracked and his face twisted with utmost, blinding joy. She had a one-second glimpse of renewed tears in his amber eyes before he dropped to his knees, wrapped his arms around her waist and pressed his face to her belly. "Yeah. I think that's okay."

Epilogue

Nine Months Later

"Shh," Hunter said. "You have to be quiet."

"I can be quiet," Kendra shouted, dancing on her toes. "I can be *very* quiet. Watch me. You'll see. Willard can be quiet, too, can't you, Willard?"

Willard began to bark.

Hunter rolled his eyes. So much for that. So much, also, for keeping the dog, his slobber, his dandruffy hair and his canine germs away. It was probably okay, though, and sometimes it was best not to fight the system. At least he'd gotten Kendra to pause in the bathroom to wash her hands after she got home from summer camp.

Okay. Here goes.

With a deep breath, he opened the nursery door and hoped for the best.

But of course he already had the best possible life, didn't he?

There she was, over in the rocking chair amidst a sea of flowers, presents and balloons, with a shaft of sunlight from the open window hitting her hair just right, shooting it through with streaks of gold. Looking up from the bundle in her lap, she caught his gaze and smiled, stopping his heart the way she always did. The way she always had, since that first day.

Livia. His wife. His life.

"Hey, guys," she said. "How was camp?"

Kendra ignored the question. Creeping forward with Willard on her heels, she accepted Livia's kiss on the cheek and peered down at the newest member of their growing family.

"Is this the baby that was in your belly?" she breathed.

"Yes," Livia said.

"What's her name?"

"Jayla Marie."

"Does she know I'm her big sister?"

Livia smoothed Kendra's hair. "Why don't you sit on my lap and tell her?"

Kendra didn't need to be asked twice. Vibrating with impatience while Livia shifted Jayla to one side, she hopped up and—it figured—insisted on holding the baby herself.

"Hi, Jayla," she cooed. "Hi, Jaaay-laaa. I'm your

sister. You have to do everything I say. And leave my dinosaurs alone, okay?"

Hunter, who'd come over to keep a closer eye on Willard, who was sniffing the baby's bare pink toes with great hope, laughed. So did Livia. Then they stared at the miracle they'd created together.

Despite all his dire warnings about being quiet so the baby could sleep, Jayla was awake, her eyes, which were an indeterminate shade somewhere between his whiskey color and Livia's hazel, focusing on Livia and then Kendra with bright interest. Her fat fists waved. Her plump legs kicked, ruffling the skirt of her little pink dress. And her perfect rosebud of a mouth curled into a smile so beautiful he didn't even care that it'd only been caused by gas.

He stared down at his girls, stricken silent with joy.

Livia, in that knowing way she had, glanced up and held his gaze. "Well, Daddy," she asked, taking his hand and squeezing it, "what do you think?"

Blinking back his sudden tears, he smiled.

"I think I'm the luckiest man in the world. That's what I think."

Willard, taking advantage of his distraction, licked Jayla's toes and then stared up at them both, his tongue dangling in clear agreement.

* * * * *

L♥VE IN THE LIMELIGHT

Fantasy, Fame and Fortune...Hollywood-Style!

Book #1
By *New York Times* and *USA TODAY*
Bestselling Author Brenda Jackson
STAR OF HIS HEART
August 2010

Book #2
By A.C. Arthur
SING YOUR PLEASURE
September 2010

Book #3
By Ann Christopher
SEDUCED ON THE RED CARPET
October 2010

Book #4
By *Essence* Bestselling Author Adrianne Byrd
LOVERS PREMIERE
November 2010

Set in Hollywood's entertainment industry,
two unstoppable sisters and their two friends
find romance, glamour and dreams-come-true.

KIMANI™
ROMANCE

www.kimanipress.com
www.myspace.com/kimanipress

REQUEST YOUR FREE BOOKS!

2 FREE NOVELS
PLUS 2 FREE GIFTS!

KIMANI™
ROMANCE

Love's ultimate destination!

YES! Please send me 2 FREE Kimani™ Romance novels and my 2 FREE gifts (gifts are worth about $10). After receiving them, if I don't wish to receive any more books, I can return the shipping statement marked "cancel." If I don't cancel, I will receive 4 brand-new novels every month and be billed just $4.69 per book in the U.S. or $5.24 per book in Canada. That's a saving of over 20% off the cover price. It's quite a bargain! Shipping and handling is just 50¢ per book.* I understand that accepting the 2 free books and gifts places me under no obligation to buy anything. I can always return a shipment and cancel at any time. Even if I never buy another book from Kimani Press, the two free books and gifts are mine to keep forever.

168/368 XDN E7PZ

Name _____ (PLEASE PRINT) _____

Address _____ Apt. # _____

City _____ State/Prov. _____ Zip/Postal Code _____

Signature (if under 18, a parent or guardian must sign)

Mail to **The Reader Service:**
IN U.S.A.: P.O. Box 1867, Buffalo, NY 14240-1867
IN CANADA: P.O. Box 609, Fort Erie, Ontario L2A 5X3

Not valid for current subscribers to Kimani Romance books.

Want to try two free books from another line?
Call 1-800-873-8635 or visit www.morefreebooks.com.

* Terms and prices subject to change without notice. Prices do not include applicable taxes. N.Y. residents add applicable sales tax. Canadian residents will be charged applicable provincial taxes and GST. Offer not valid in Quebec. This offer is limited to one order per household. All orders subject to approval. Credit or debit balances in a customer's account(s) may be offset by any other outstanding balance owed by or to the customer. Please allow 4 to 6 weeks for delivery. Offer available while quantities last.

Your Privacy: Kimani Press is committed to protecting your privacy. Our Privacy Policy is available online at www.eHarlequin.com or upon request from the Reader Service. From time to time we make our lists of customers available to reputable third parties who may have a product or service of interest to you. If you would prefer we not share your name and address, please check here. ☐

Help us get it right—We strive for accurate, respectful and relevant communications. To clarify or modify your communication preferences, visit us at www.ReaderService.com/consumerschoice.

KROM10R